Shadow of the
NINJA

AF702486

Shadow of the NINJA

Katsumi Toda

Published by
dragon books

ISBN 0 946062 00 5 Library of Congress Catalogue Card No. 82-071143

"THE SHADOW OF THE WARRIOR
HOLDS THE SPIRIT OF THE NINJA"
(from the secret scrolls of the Tomokatsu Ryu)

SHADOW OF THE NINJA

Acknowledgements

Lesley Anne Copp-Taylor/Editor
Malcolm Copp-Taylor/Line drawings & photography
Garry O'Keefe B.A. (Hons.)/Layout & design
Haruko Chambers/Special translation

Library of Congress Catalogue Card No. 82.071143
I.S.B.N. 0 946062 005

Printed in Great Britain
by The Anchor Press Ltd. Tiptree, Essex
First published June 1982
Second impression October 1982

Distributed in the USA
by Sakura/Dragon Corp. Los Angeles, California

© Katsumi Toda 1982

Contents

Blood in the dust

CHAPTER ONE

BLOOD IN THE DUST

Death was soon to visit the stubble field. A crowd gathered, jostling for the best view. Stones from the low stone wall fell – breaking the eerie silence. As the crowd surged the wall broke with a crack and more stones tumbled into the dusty soil.

The noise of all this did not disturb the two men who faced each other in the centre of the field.

They stood about three feet apart, facing each other squarely. The two men bore the distinctive clothes of the samurai – the hakama, which, under pain of death was their privilege, also they had the right to bear swords.

They faced each other eyeball to eyeball, swords rested in scabbards. No silly threats or tricks, this was reality, one would live and one would die.

The crowd murmured and became restless at the seeming inaction, but no one dared speak aloud, for samurai law said that the peasant was the property of the samurai class. His life depended upon the samurai's good favour. However, one or two of the more enterprising peasants were laying bets at the outcome.

Back in the field of honour, the two men remained motionless, subtly probing each other with the power of the mind. Small traps were set and sprung, but both men were equally matched.

A cool breeze began to blow, ruffling the top knots of the samurai – then with dazzling speed – the final conflict.

Both drew their swords. To the absorbed onlookers it seemed that both must surely be fatally cut. But one was cut deeper, this was Ai-uchi the simultaneous strike, the truth of the sword.

Slowly, as if in a dream, one of the samurai wavered from his posture and with a faint smile of resignation and respect – fell. He was dead before he hit the ground, the resting place of the true warrior. His heart had been cut through.

The wind fluttered his kimono around the vertical slash which opened his soul to his ancestors. Now a purple, brown patch of his life blood was spreading into a pool around him, gently seeping into the rough earth as in so many other places, so many other times before. For samurai life was obligation unto death – honour in the face of death.

The samurai who remained standing, whom some would call, the victorious one, gazed down with soft eyes at the man who was now at peace. He looked at the red slash down his sword blade and then back to the fallen man. He bowed slightly, so slightly that the onlookers could not see, for this was samurai honour, peasants could not understand.

Simultaneous strike

The samurai drew a piece of soft paper from within the folds of his kimono and thoroughly wiped his blade clean. When he was satisfied he slowly returned his sword to its scabbard. Not as some showmen who throw their swords back into their scabbards – to impress fools. Only then did the samurai check his own wound. His kimono was sliced through with a horizontal cut, the material was damp with his own blood, he had been cut, but not deeply. His battlefield training told him what he must do now.

He returned his gaze to the field and to the area where the villagers were gathered.

"Listen to me!" his voice boomed out. The villagers bowed their heads, for it was unthinkable to look at a samurai whilst he spoke to you.

The samurai continued, looking for the strongest-willed villager, he found him by the way he stood and directed his voice to that man.

"Listen to me, all of you. I have honourably killed this man in fair fight. Soon men will come to view this place. None of you will come to this fallen man, none of you will try to rob his body. I shall know if you disobey and I shall return to make this a village of widows."

He paused "You understand?" Silence. But the silence was enough to prove their fear of samurai revenge.

The samurai strode forward, as he neared the gap in the recently breached stone wall, the crowd parted, giving him a respectful distance. The samurai seemed not to notice them as he moved forward with one purpose.

He walked down the narrow path until he reached the outskirts of the village. It was the usual sort of shabby farming community. Narrow lanes between the shabby buildings, from whose eaves drying vegetables hung ready for pickling.

The samurai paused in mid stride and sensed the air. He moved his head slightly from side to side until he heard the sound he was listening for. Then he turned in that direction.

As he picked his way towards the small hut behind what passed as a main street, the sound grew louder. Now it was recognisable as hammer blows against iron followed by a hiss as water quenched the hot metal.

The hut was simple, charcoal and wood piled neatly to one side. The entrance was a simple garden, beautiful but simple, the plants tended with great skill. This place was different from the rest of the village, but it nestled in its very heart, as a beautiful flower amongst weeds.

The samurai drew close to the entrance and with quiet, respectful words said, "Excuse me, may I enter?" There was a pause in the rhythm of hammering and quenching.

"Enter with respect," came the reply. The samurai removed his long sword and placed it in the sword rack, thoughtfully placed before the entrance. This did not leave the samurai defenceless. He still, as custom allowed, wore the broad bladed dirk. Anyway, the long sword was difficult to use indoors.

Bowing slightly, as a mark of respect, the samurai entered. The interior was dark save for the glow of the fire.

The samurai's manner was formal. Here was no villager, no ordinary peasant, this was the master of iron. He who knew the mysteries of earth, air, water, fire and iron – a swordsmith.

The swordsmith was an old man, dressed entirely in white with a small black cap tied firmly on his head – the mark of the master of iron. This was a sacred place, drawn away from the world.

In one corner sat his hammerman. A young man also dressed in white, an apprentice swordsmith who had effectively given his life to his master. The hammerman held the long-handled hammer carefully, watching and waiting lest any disrespect be shown to his master.

Sensing his pupil's uneasiness the sword master looked into the samurai's heart.

"At your ease Muroto, this man is of good heart."

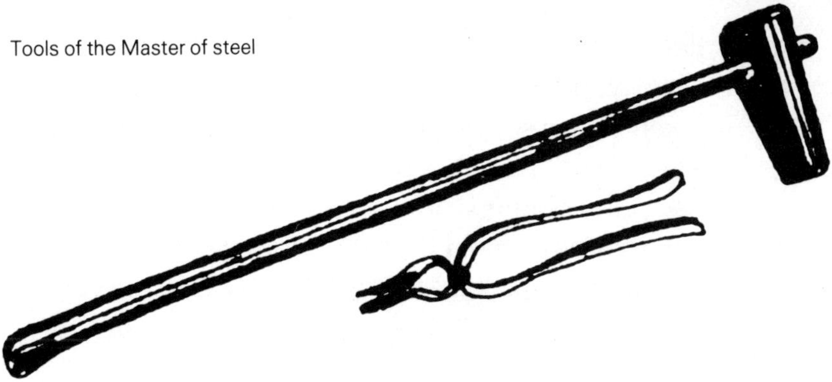

Tools of the Master of steel

The assistant relaxed and put the hammer, which two villagers could not lift, lightly at his side.

"So samurai," said the master of iron, "you are alive and the other is dead!"

"You know of our duel?"

"Yes I sensed the battle."

"Then you sense also that it was honourable."

The swordsmith looked long and cold at the samurai but did not answer. In matters of such depth, answers are not necessary.

"Tend your wound samurai."

With a slight bow, the samurai opened his kimono. He now saw the extent of his wound. It was about six inches long, perfectly horizontal, just above his right nipple and gently pulsing with blood.

The swordsmith made a sign to his assistant, then took a pair of long-handled tongs from a rack and drew a piece of iron rod from the fire, it glowed yellow-white in the darkness. The assistant handed the tongs to the samurai. The samurai prepared himself and brought the hot iron close to his chest.

"Wait – the colour of the iron is not right," the swordsmith gently said, "let the colour become that of the three day moon."

The samurai paused, the iron cooled.

"Now is the time, work swiftly with strong spirit."

The samurai drew the iron to his chest and pressed it

into his flesh. There was a searing hiss of the blood vapourized and the wound was cauterized.

The pain was intense, the samurai made no sound.

"Take the kimono off and Muroto will repair it."

The samurai obeyed, he handed the kimono jacket to the assistant who received it with a slight bow of respect.

"Now go and wash at the well." The samurai bowed, then without turning, he backed out of the hut.

The Master of steel

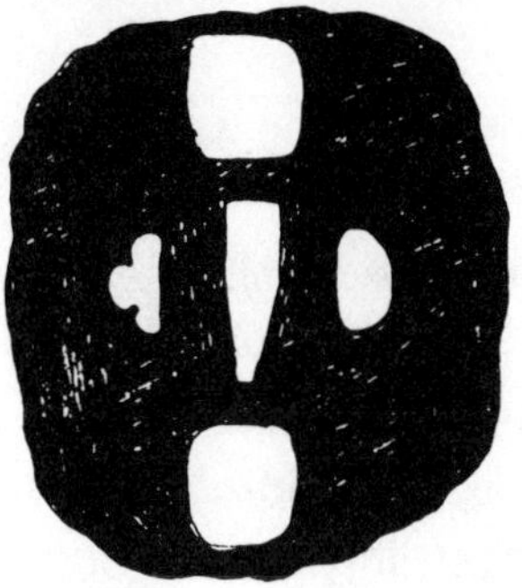

Sword guard

Ippon Sugi Nobori (tree climber)

He walked to the well, drew a bucket of water and carefully cleansed the wound. With a long length of white cotton material he dressed the cut.

His body was strong, schooled in the martial ways since boyhood.

Pausing the samurai looked up. Something disturbed him but he could not tell what it was. From the hut the hammer blows began again.

High up in the trees a figure lay silently. Dressed from head to foot in black, a ninja spy of the Tomokatsu Ryu. He had observed the duel and followed the samurai to this place. The samurai was well in range of his bow but his orders were strict "observe and report". He saw that this samurai was a strong fighter, aged about 45. His masters would need more information but he could not approach any closer. He knew the uncanny power of the samurai's "sixth sense".

Then it came – the thing he waited for – the samurai turned his back on the ninja. His back was tattooed with a figure of the war god Hachiman – the result of a youthful mistake and too much sake. He bore the mark of his youth, but now mature he did not make such errors.

The swordsmith's assistant came out from the hut and gave the samurai his kimono. The samurai put it on. The assistant then handed him a plain wooden box about four inches square.

"My master has no need to speak with you again but wishes you to accept this."

The samurai opened the box. It contained a simple iron sword guard, still warm from its final quenching. Made from the bar of iron used to cauterize the samurai's wound. Punched into its surface was the simple message "eternal vigilance". The samurai looked up, something was wrong.

The ninja was gone from the tree, bearing the knowledge his master needed to find the samurai whenever he wished. A wound on his chest and the tattoo of the war god Hachiman on his back.

CHAPTER TWO

DARK RECKONINGS

By the time the samurai had prepared himself to leave the swordsmith's hut, his secret watcher was many miles away. Dressed as a travelling priest he made his way across country, keeping well away from roads and pathways. Should he have been challenged by a border patrol, he would have appeared totally innocent and without weapons. But the truth was that one end of the six foot long staff which he carried contained a straight-bladed sword, which in turn fitted into the end of the staff and became a long bladed halberd, enough to take a man from his horse. The buddhist rosary which he wore over one shoulder contained compressed smoke flares and explosive grenades. These were made to a formula stolen by the third generation master of the Tomokatsu Ryu two hundred years before. The story was as interesting now as when the children of the ninja clan were told of it.

The third generation master made a trip to the great mainland of China. There, under the orders of the Lord of Sado Island he made his way to the forbidden city and assassinated the Prince Chia, whose pirate fleet had been raiding Sado Island for years. In making his escape he managed to steal the records of the Imperial Fireworks master. The Chinese saw only entertainment in the flashes and explosions, but to the master of the Tomokatsu Ryu Ninja here was a secret weapon which the ninja had made into a fine art over the two hundred years they had possessed it.

The travelling priest carried a laquered box on his back, which in the normal order of things would be a small shrine. But for the ninja priest the travelling shrine housed poisons

The travelling priest

The priest is not all he seems

and his bow and arrows carefully disassembled. The figure of Kwannon, the goddess of mercy, was made of the same compressed explosive as his rosary. And the simple incense sticks were fuses, graded by colour from ten seconds to one hour. His reddish black ninja camouflage suit was folded carefully into a buddhist sutra scroll. The sleeves of his robes contained many small pockets where the shuriken throwing stars were hidden. Around his waist was the ten thousand power chain – the manrikikusari, which in his skilled hands could break a sword blade or create a whirling defence to block the flight of an enemy's arrow. Thus it was, that the seemingly helpless priest crossed the two provinces in two days and nights. He did not sleep or eat. When fatigue and hunger came, he used the secret kankuji mind controlling techniques and trudged on in the ecstasy of pain.

On the morning of the third day he reached the mountainous land where the ninja stronghold was situated.

In the low valley was a tiny unprotected farming village. Here the trade of the ninja stronghold was carried out. The dyers, the picklers, the sake brewers and woodcarvers were all ninja. Strangers were watched carefully, and if suspect, silently killed and disposed of without trace.

The ten thousand power chain

Blow pipe and darts

Explosive arrow

Once, long ago, a band of masterless samurai, Ronin, had tried to terrorize the village, hoping for easy sport. They rode into the village and demanded the village headman. Within thirty seconds, the horsemen fell, pierced by poison arrows and blow darts. Smoothly and quietly the bodies and horses were removed. When the second wave of horsemen galloped in as the supposedly surprise attack, they found an empty village – forty two seconds later, the village was again deserted. The rear guard on the main road were despatched quietly by black clad ninja using the ten thousand power chain.

The entire area of the village was criss-crossed by a series of tunnels and bolt-holes. Incendiary devices were hidden, which could convert the village into a fireball at a moment's notice.

Passing through the village, the ninja priest paused at certain points, which told the ninja security that all had gone well. Had he not paused or paused too long – the security would know that there was a problem, and would have taken appropriate action.

With the path clear, the ninja priest passed through the village and up the mountain valley. He passed training areas

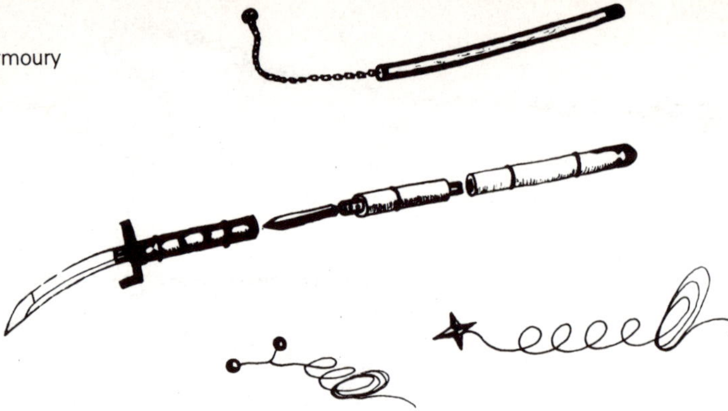

The priest's armoury

where ninja practised a variety of secret techniques. Most interesting was the area where ninja attack groups practised their assassination techniques. Special movable straw palisades could be used to mimic the grounds and interior of a castle, based on information from ninja intelligence squads. The exact position of doorways and Yojimbo bodyguards could be plotted enabling the ninja attack force to make a dummy run of their actions.

Although the ninja priest passed members of his training group, they did not acknowledge his arrival, nor he them. For they knew he must marshall his memory and enter a self-hypnotised state where he would have total recall of all details of his mission. Even the most minor point could be of great importance in the planning of the action.

He passed by the area where the ninjas' children were schooled in the rudiments of their craft. For who would suspect a small child of four or five of being a threat. But the "little innocents" as they were nicknamed, could transport vital messages or explosive presents.

The ninja priest swiftly passed this area, he was nearing his de-briefing and with each step he cleared a part of his mind. The tricks of mind control which could enable a captured ninja to withstand the harshest torture until sweet relief came from his comrade's arrow, were now being used to calm the mind, forget physical discomfort and prepare for total recall.

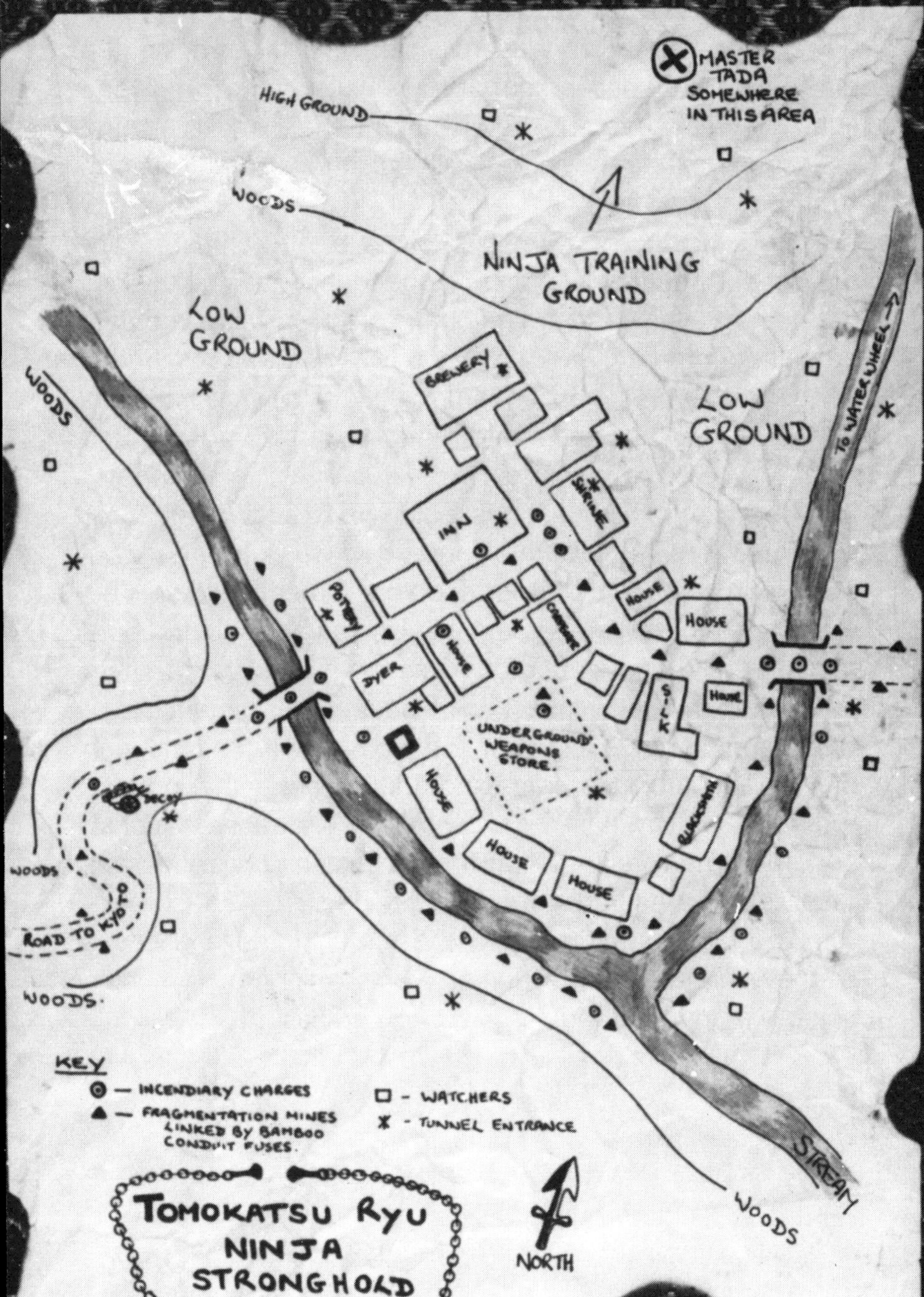

MASTER TADA SOMEWHERE IN THIS AREA
HIGH GROUND
WOODS
NINJA TRAINING GROUND
LOW GROUND
LOW GROUND
TO WATER WHEEL
WOODS
BREWERY
INN
SHRINE
POTTERY
HOUSE
HOUSE
DYER
HOUSE
SILK
HOUSE
UNDERGROUND WEAPONS STORE.
HOUSE
HOUSE
HOUSE
BLACKSMITH
WOODS
ROAD TO KYOTO
WOODS.
KEY
— INCENDIARY CHARGES
— FRAGMENTATION MINES LINKED BY BAMBOO CONDUIT FUSES.
— WATCHERS
— TUNNEL ENTRANCE
STREAM
WOODS
TOMOKATSU RYU NINJA STRONGHOLD
NORTH

The priest entered a small cleft in the rocks, which from a mere ten feet away was invisible. He walked down the dimly lit corridor hacked out of rock. Following carefully the lines of weakness and hewn out of the living rock, the passage was proof against all but the strongest earth tremor.

Ninja science had also evolved a further safeguard against earthquakes. A simple stone font containing thick oil had a small oiled paper boat floating on its surface. The boat contained mercury, and when earth tremors reached a dangerous level, the boat overflowed with oil and sank. This signified that it was the right time to leave the underground hideaway. Simple but effective.

Soon the ninja priest passed down to a lower level, far away from the natural light. Here the air was kept fresh by a system of bamboo tubes connected to a great bellows. This was primed by a water wheel, fed by a subterranean mountain stream. This masterpiece was yet another of the third generation master's collection of ideas, in this instance, one taken from the gold mines of Kai. A pity about Lord Shingen of the Takeda clan, a brave and honourable man who died too soon, but at least he did not see his generals perish under the merciless musket fire at Nagashino, directly as a result of ninja espionage.

The ninja priest entered the room at the end of his journey. Tiredness and hunger were banished. His whole being was primed and ready for total recall.

CHAPTER THREE

IN THE HALL OF MEMORY

In the memory room, as it was known, everything was painted white. This was the code for total recall, so sophisticated was the science of ninja mind control, that a square of white paper could be used to help a ninja remember secret directions when on a journey.

The ninja priest sat down, his heels tucked well under. He still bore his staff and portable shrine. He would not discard these items until the ordeal of total recall was over. Their possession was an important part of the mind trick.

In front of him was a low white table, on it a large oblong of jet black paper, by its side a brush and freshly prepared ink. The ninja would write the details on the paper in a precise order, as both paper and ink were black, nothing could disturb his concentration. There was no room or reason for any personal attachment to his experiences, simply cold total recall.

Later the journal could be read after immersion in horse urine which oxidised the black to a legible brown-red. Thus the account was eventually passed to the inquisition who held the hand of ninja strategy and who would advise on the best mode of action.

The priest raised the brush from the white table. Staring straight ahead of him, his eyes glazed and he began to write swiftly, at no time did he even glance at the sheet of black paper. Soon the task was finished. The brush was placed on the ink stand. Holding the staff in his left hand, he rose and walked out of the white room.

He walked down a long corrdior and eventually entered another dimly lit room. The only colour in the room was that of the natural rock. Here was a large basket on a low table, he opened the lid of the basket and drew out his own clothes. The ninja priest removed all his priestly garments. Naked, he picked up his own bundle and walked to a dark corner where a bath had been prepared. He thoroughly washed himself then stepped into the deep bath tub. He relaxed here for about twenty minutes, then got out, dried himself and put on his own clothes. He then left by a small door.

From here he entered a comfortable room, at one side of which was freshly-prepared onigiri – rice balls wrapped in thin slivers of seaweed. The ninja sat down and began to eat. He drank deeply of a special tea infusion, specially formulated to give renewed energy.

When his meal was finished he drew back the cover of the futon matress and lay down. He slept soundly – without dreams.

Whilst he slept, the ninja inquisitors were analysing his account of his mission.

A small bell rang in the ninja's room. His eyes immediately opened, he rose up, fully clothed. The two inquisitors entered and began the debriefing process. They both had a copy of the ninja's statement.

Subtly probing, softly questioning and re-questioning they carried on until fully satisfied that they had all possible answers. Then they rose and left to present their report to the master of the Tomokatsu Ryu.

The shape of memory

Lock pick

Yari-spearhead

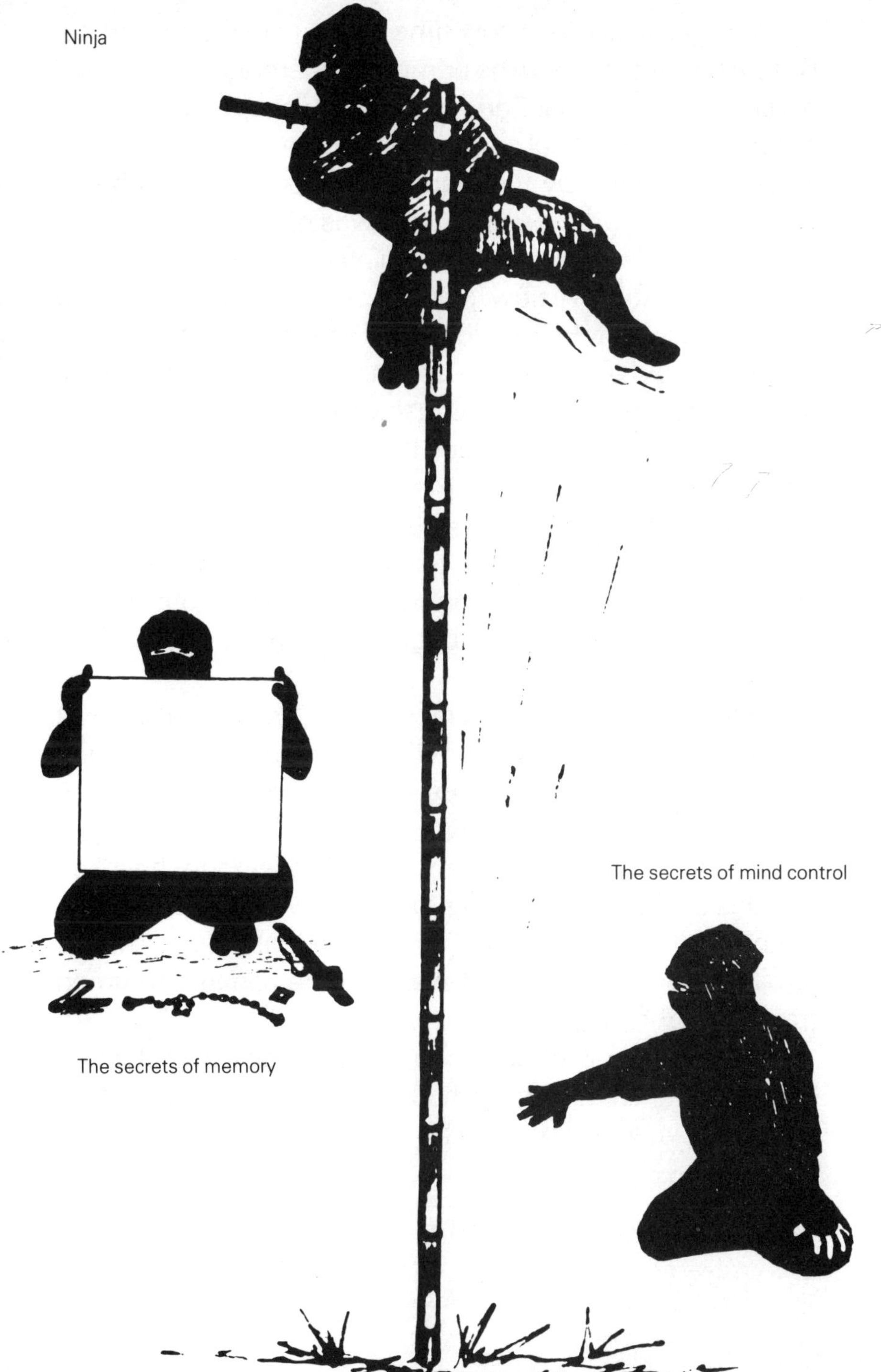
The secrets of mind control
The secrets of memory

For the ninja it was now time to return to his normal life. Before leaving the room he primed his memory to remove all details of the mission. Performing the Kankuji hand signs he entered a state of cool contemplation. He picked up a small laquered tube left by the inquisitors. Opening the tube he withdrew a roll of thin paper. On it was printed two Chinese characters – the positioning of which would be the code for erasing memory. A new pattern of characters was used after each separate mission thus ensuring that no trace memory could ever occur. After gazing at the characters for a few moments the ninja folded the paper and placed it in the flame of a candle. The paper flared and was quickly consumed to ashes. As the flame grew and then died, so all memory of his mission was burned away.

In a trance-like state the ninja rose and left the room. He again passed through the long corridors and then out into the light. His eyes blinked in the brightness of the last rays of the evening sun.

The whole process had taken ten hours. There did exist a rapid method which gave total recall in less than one hour, but it risked the sanity of the user and was only used at times when swift action was vital.

As he passed down the valley to the village, he joked with his comrades practising for their own sport or relaxing watching the training. Soon he reached his house and his family. Nothing was said, it was as if he had just returned from a neighbourly call.

The ninja picked up the piece of wood which he had been carving when the call had come from the master. He settled down and picking up his chisel began to work on the wood.

CHAPTER FOUR

SHADOW OF THE WIND

"Kill me! If you dare!" The wild eyes of the young man spoke of madness. His sword was drawn, it flashed from side to side.

"I have no quarrel with you" said the old man. He was a retired samurai who had fought long and well in the service of his lord. Now he had laid his sword to rest and retired to seclusion, awaiting his end.

"Kill me! If you dare!" said the young man again. He flashed and weaved his sword in crazy erratic arcs. His clothes, though tattered, were clearly those of a samurai, but on him they did not quite fit. The old samurai noticed this and wondered. Keeping a safe distance, he backed down the narrow road cut through the bamboo grove. With each crazy step the young man took, the old one backed away.

In this fashion they entered an overgrown part of the path. Huge bamboo stalks stretched to the sky. They swayed, making a gentle creaking sound. Peasants said that this was the language of the dead who took the bamboo as their meeting place.

The path was dappled dark and light as the sun fought its way to the ground below. With resignation the old man knew there was a limit to his backward process, for samurai ethic dictated – "be strong in the service of your lord, but be gentle in your daily affairs."

Only fools and madmen pick quarrels, fools are best left to their delusions, but madmen are most dangerous – like a crazy dog terrorizing a farmer's livestock, they must be dealt with.

The young man came on, his sword flashing from side

to side. Belonging to no recognisable sword school, the technique was thus infinitely unpredictable and infinitely deadly.

The old samurai sized up the situation. The reason for the confrontation? Ludicrous – passing by on the bamboo lined road, the young man had called out, "Well met, brother samurai." As honour dictated, the old samurai had remained silent, but the young man had taken this politeness as an insult and had drawn his sword.

The old samurai pondered the final decision – the seal was set upon what was to happen next. As the crazy young man weaved and circled, his attempt at tying the chomage – the topknot that marked the samurai for life – came adrift and his hair cascaded around his face and in his eyes – which burned with madness, twin pools of venom.

"You old dog, think I am not good enough for you? Let me tell you, I am just as proud as you samurai curs. I do not fear your tricks!" The young man shrieked out this message, foaming at the mouth. As he spat the words, trickles of saliva dripped down his chin and onto his kimono leaving dark stains.

The old samurai played the final card in this deadly game –

"When did you leave the farm young man? For I know your heart, you are no samurai, the clothes you wear and the sword you bear are not yours. You have robbed the body of a samurai warrior, did you also murder him?"

"It is not murder, you samurai are the fleas on the backs of us farmers, I would crush you all!" The young man's fury was reaching the point of greatest danger.

"I am not armed" the old samurai softly said, his backward movement ended.

"Then die like a dog, I will cut your heart out and eat it!"

The young man made to cut at the samurai, not realising that the distance and timing were both wrong. The sword flashed down to where he thought the old man's neck

should be, and encountered only air. The old samurai, agile as a cat had moved close in, his hand formed into a fist. His forearm struck the nerve centre on the young man's sword arm. As a reflex the young man's fingers jerked open and the sword spun in deadly circles, finally thudding into the trunk of one of the huge bamboo stalks where it quivered from side to side, flashing bright then dark as the sun caught its polished surface.

At the same time as the old man's forearm caught his opponent's sword arm, his toes, bunched up to make a spear point, thudded into the soft area under the mad one's breast bone. The crazy eyes widened as the nerve shock overloaded his brain. The force of the kick lifted him slightly off his feet. Closing the distance quickly, the old samurai took the outstretched sword arm and lifted the madman up, around and over, dropping to the half crouch known as iai goshi as the madman flew in the air. At the decisive moment, the old samurai drew his hands down as if cutting with a sword and the body was stopped in its motion by the rocky path. A sharp click as the neck and many of the spinal vertebrae shattered was the only sound.

The decisive moment

The farmer's son was dead. Killed by a technique that centuries later would be developed into the famous Shi ho nage, the four directions throw of Aikido masters.

The pitiful bundle, that seconds before had been a fireball of fury, twitched slightly as nerve endings died, blood trickled from the ears. It was devastating, terrible to watch, but necessary for madness was catching.

As the old man rose from the position of iai goshi, the secret of the sword way, he sensed a watching presence, but one without threat. Looking in the direction of his observer he saw a samurai, aged about forty-five, with a roughly sewn horizontal gash on his kimono. The newcomer bowed in the samurai manner.

"Please excuse the necessity of speaking to you, I journey this way and by accident I have observed this debt of honour."

The old man considered the heart behind these words, "No matter, I trust your words to be true."

"Master," said the man, who beneath his kimono bore a tattoo of the war god Hachiman on his back and a newly cauterized wound on his chest, "Fate has brought us to this place and to this meeting. I am on important business following a just cause. Please excuse my impoliteness, please teach me your way."

The old man gazed hard and then spoke, "To learn the way takes many years of soft study."

"I only have weeks master."

"Then the way will be hard and you may die."

"Please accept me as your pupil."

The old man turned and walked away. The samurai followed.

Tetsu keibo

CHAPTER FIVE

TURN OF THE TIDE

The large green melon shattered with the force of the weighted chain, spraying its red heart in all directions. The ninja master whirled and circled in the intricate movements of the ten thousand power chain. Gathered around him were six of his most senior ninja. Each held a melon, one by one in no particular order, they would throw their melons high or low in the direction of their master.

He was dressed in the complete battle equipment of reddish, black kimono and loose breeches tied below the knee. On his feet he wore the ankle length, split-toed jika tabi shoes. His head was covered with the same reddish black material. He appeared like his own shadow, dark and ominous. Strapped to his back was the single-edged, straight bladed sword. [Shorter than the curved swords which the samurai regarded as his soul]. To the ninja the sword was a tool, no more important than any of his other weapons and survival tools. The scabbard was a dull black laquer, longer than the blade, its end was packed with a powder which could be blown in the face of an enemy before either the sword, shuriken throwing star or ten thousand power chain finished the task. This uniform was standard issue amongst the various ninja groups who held no political or clear allegiance, only allegiance to the highest bidder.

The ninja master slowed his technique, then speeded it up as he felt the movement in the void – as ninja science referred to the art of the sixth sense. The master was most accomplished in this field of study. So accomplished that he practised the melon exercise with a blindfold. Eyeless he sensed for the next attack. The melon came low and from the rear – the chain whirled and the fruit exploded. Almost instantly two other melons came high and low from left and right. The chain left his hand and snaked towards its target. The ninja master reached behind for his sword which cut as it drew; so precise was the ninja master's control of the void that as the thrown chain crushed its way into the highest melon, the sword sliced through the lower melon. Two down, two to go.

Silence, then the master felt the direction of the remaining two – their force stronger than the other four. The fifth melon flew straight at the sword master, in the secret art of Tomokatsu Ryu, he jumped high in the air. Catching the melon between his knees he pressed inwards and struck the fruit with his left fist, the fruit caved in. This technique was designed to be used against an unarmed man running forwards. The knee smash would take the ears and the hammer fist, the weak spot at the crown of the head, resulting in death.

As the ninja master landed, the sixth and last melon came low from slightly left. The left hand, still wet from the melon juice, drew a throwing spike from a long pocket in the thigh of his breeches. It hissed towards the melon and struck it squarely.

Six melons gone, as the master relaxed slightly his sixth sense took over. His sword flashed and the square of silk, thrown by one of his assistants as a test for his master, fluttered in two. The ninja master tore off his blindfold and finding the culprit, gave him a good-natured cuff across the side of the head.

"Try to fool your old master, eh? Kichibei." The assistants face reddened slightly, then the master laughed,

"Maybe next time!"

Although a senior in technique, Kichibei was young in years and had the recklessness of his youth. His missions were carefully chosen for him to avoid this youthful impetu-

Forest training

ousness.

"Master Tada."

The young Kichibei stepped forward, offering a cotton towel for his master to wipe the sweat and melon juice. In his heart the master Tada revelled in the unpredictable nature of his younger ninja – always trying to test their master. In a way they were his teachers, for they taught him not to relax in the knowledge of his advanced technique.

"Master Tada?" The young man spoke again.

"How did you know that the silk cloth would come?"

Tada laughed.

"How did I know? I did not know!"

Kichibei looked puzzled.

"There is no knowing when you enter the void. If you try to force the power, it will rebound upon you. There is no knowing, only action. And if you know there are ten attackers, treat it as a hundred attackers, then you cannot be fooled into thinking that you have reached the end. For there can be no end."

"Look!" Tada exclaimed, "There!"

He pointed up to the trees, Kichibei looked up, only to receive a second cuff across his head.

"More study, don't be fooled, there are traps in all things. Now I have important business to attend to Kichibei."

"Master Tada?"

"You need more practice. Spend the rest of your training session finding all the melon seeds."

The young Kichibei's eyes widened as he viewed the forest glade where training had taken place. The ground was covered by last year's leaf fall, the melon seeds were widely scattered. His comrades, who until now had kept their silence, burst out laughing.

"And the rest of you, practice your bowmanship."

The master Tada turned and walked to his cave entrance, a slight smile on his lips.

He untied his sword scabbard and left it at the cave

The Master Tada

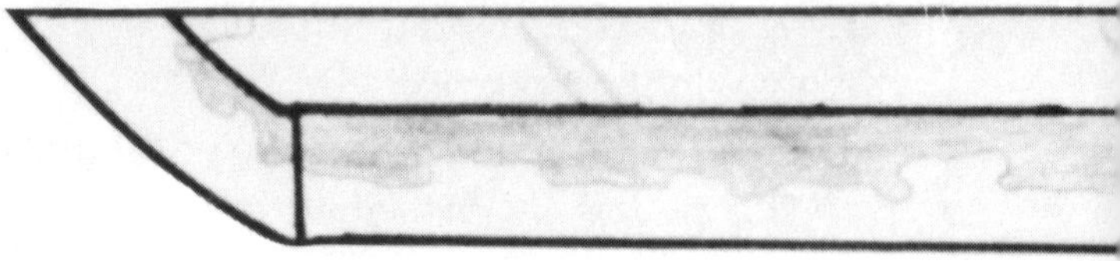

The edge of the Ninja sword

entrance. His assistants would collect the weapons he had used and clean them.

Tada walked down the rough hewn corridor, where earlier the ninja who dressed as a priest, had been debriefed. He came to his own quarters and removing his battle uniform, put on his favourite kimono. This garment was a subtle blue colour and was part payment for services rendered to the house of the Kanda prostitutes in nearby Kyoto. The madame of the Kanda house had been battered by a petty official who demanded much more than the accepted bribe. Rather than pay this, the madame had commisioned the Tomokatsu Ninja to engineer an embarassing situation which removed the petty official in disgrace. The ninja treated anyone's money with respect, there was no class distinction amongst ninja – money spoke, regardless of its accent.

Tada wrapped the fine grey silk obi around his waist, he tied it neatly. He sat down behind the low table. On the plain cryptomeria wood table was a small bronze bell with a classical "vajra" thunder bolt as its handle. Tada picked the bell up and rang it once. The soft tinkle echoed sweetly

The Ninja sword

down the stone corridors. A space of half a minute and the ninja inquisitors shuffled up the passageway – they entered, bowing slightly.

"Be seated!"

The two sat down, they wore dark brown kimono, very plain. Both had copies of the ninja priest's statement and the results of their questioning.

"So Kikushujo," said Tada to the more senior,

"What news?"

The man known as Kikushujo was in his late fifties, totally bald with a prison brand on the side of his skull. The mark of an early mission, which he would bear to the grave. Unlike the ninja priest who used the technique of forgetfulness – Kikushijo bore a reminder, so he could never go out on active service again. But his skill as an inquisitor was great and his contribution to the ninja group was much respected.

"Master Tada, we have studied the information received. This is our man, we still do not know his name, but the trick with the sword marks him out as the man we seek. The trick, or secret art was the reason the samurai won the duel. Instead of wearing his sword with the cutting edge uppermost, he wore it reversed. Therefore, instead of drawing with the right hand and cutting horizontally, the samurai drew with his left hand and striking vertically used the rotation of his hips, his right fist on the back of his sword blade to cut deep, to sever the heart of his opponent.

Our information reveals him to have a tattoo of Hachiman Dai Bosatsu on his back."

Tada looked up – it was out of character with such a fine swordsman. It may show the way to a secret weakness, Tada marked the point in his mind for future reference.

"Continue" said Tada.

The inquisitor Kikushujo began to lay down the information necessary to plan the demise the Hachiman samurai.

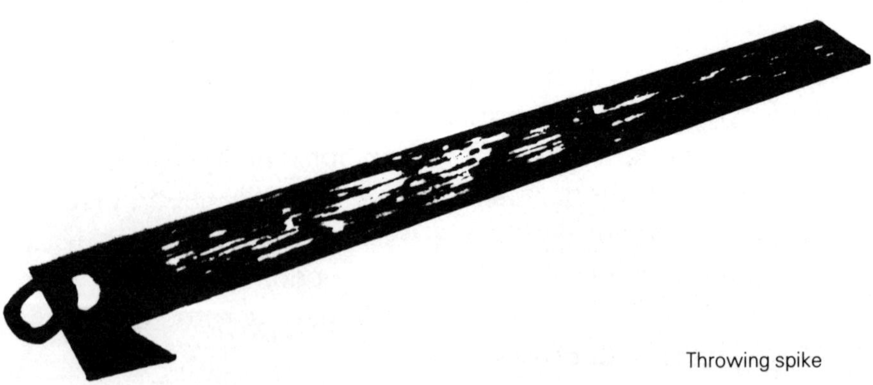

Throwing spike

CHAPTER SIX

THE AWAKENING

The world turned upside down for the hundredth time as the Hachiman samurai flew through the air. The rough, carved wooden practice sword spun out of his hands and he landed with a mighty thud on the straw bales which served as a protection against the hard forest floor. The samurai rose to his feet, picking pieces of straw out of his hair.

"Master" said the samurai, "I still do not see the point where my balance is broken."

The old samurai master picked up the wooden practice sword. He tossed it to the Hachiman samurai who caught it lightly.

"Attack again, full force" the master said.

Join me for some tea

The way of tea

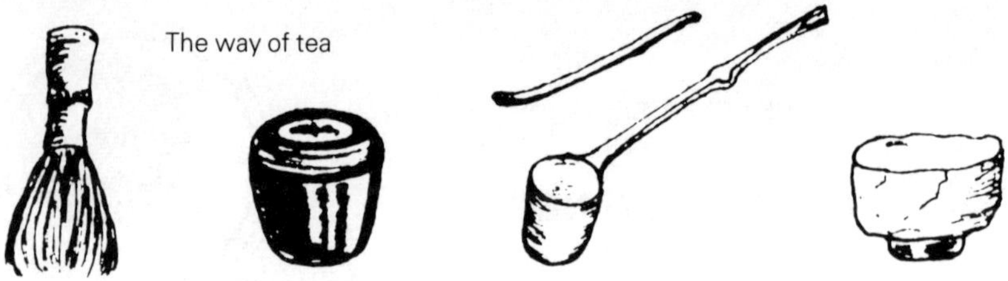

The Hachiman samurai rushed in. In a flash, the old master flipped his opponent. As his feet left the ground, the Hachiman samurai exclaimed, "Yes, I understand."

He thudded to the ground.

Enough for today", said the master, "Join me for some tea."

Without waiting for a reply the master turned and walked towards the simple hut which nestled amongst the great trees in the old forest, old as the Gods.

Pausing to remove his straw sandals the old master entered the hut. The Hachiman samurai followed, again picking bits of straw out of his clothing and hair.

Bowing slightly, the samurai also removed his sandals and entered the hut.

The inside was dimly lit by a lamp in one corner. On one wall was a rack where the old master kept his favourite weapons. A long sword, a short sword, a spear and a long curved bladed naginata halberd. The old master rarely practised with these weapons now, for his technique was far beyond them.

The master crouched in front of a small charcoal brazier on which was an iron kettle. The water, reaching boiling point hissed and bubbled. Removing the iron cover, the old

Spearpoint

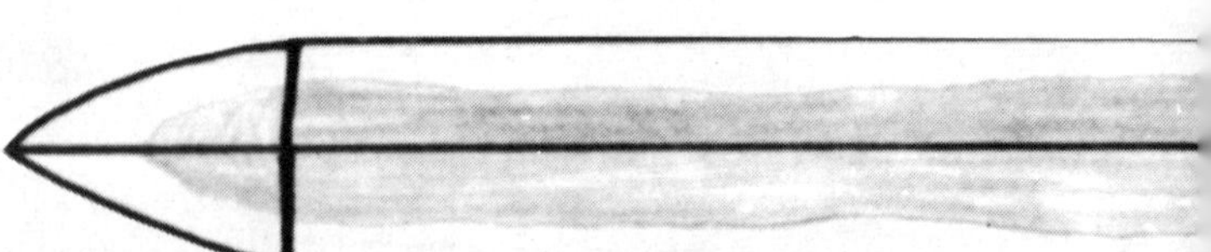

master dipped a long-handled bamboo cup into the hot water. He drew the steaming liquid out and ladled it into an old rough pottery bowl. He placed the dipper on the top of the iron kettle and picked up a black laquered tub. Removing the lid, which bore the family crest of his old clan in gold laquer, he spooned a small amount of bright green tea powder. He tapped the bamboo spatula on the side of the tea bowl and with a delicate bamboo whisk, foamed the tea with a rapid circular motion. When he was satisfied, he placed the whisk on a plain wooden tray. Picking the teabowl up in both hands, he passed it to the Hachiman samurai.

Bowing slightly the Hachiman samurai accepted the teabowl and placing it to his lips, he drank the invigorating brew. He wiped the edge from which he had drunk, then passed it back to the old master. He drank the remains and silently placed the cup to one side. He looked long and hard at the Hachiman samurai.

Silence prevailed, for what seemed an age, then breaking the peace, the Hachiman samurai spoke

"Master, as you know, my time is short, so I must disregard the politeness of samurai manners."

The old master remained silent.

Naginata with cover

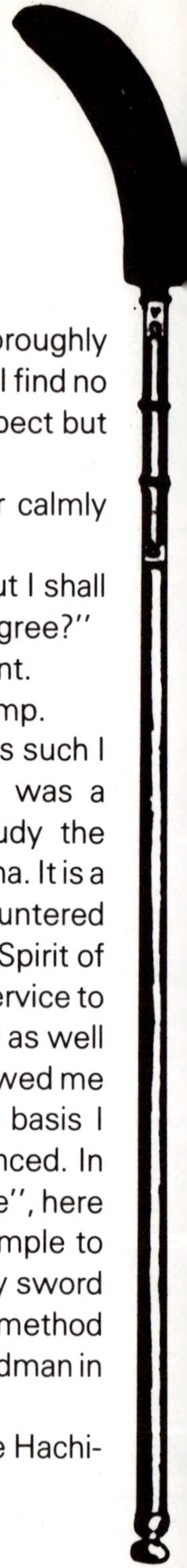

"Master" the samurai began again, "I have thoroughly studied the close fighting method of Kumi-Uchi, but I find no similarity in your method. Please forgive the disrespect but where did you develop these techniques from?"

The old samurai master pondered his answer calmly and long, then spoke –

"I shall tell you the history of my special skill but I shall require a truthful answer to one question – do you agree?"

The Hachiman samurai indicated his agreement.

The old master gazed into the flame of the lamp.

"In my youth, I was a strong swordsman and as such I became the Yojimbo bodyguard of my lord. He was a learned man whose choice was to travel to study the classics. We made a trip to the great mainland of China. It is a vast and interesting country. It was here that I encountered the grand master Hua, whose school was named "Spirit of the wind." In the course of my travels I rendered a service to the Hua family – they tried to pay me, but you know as well as I the value of money. Instead the master Hua showed me the principles of the spirit of the wind. From this basis I developed the techniques which you have experienced. In my youth my study was sword and spear – as you see", here he gestured to the weapon rack. "It seemed so simple to apply these principles of the spirit of the wind to my sword and spear. From these came the close fighting method which as you witnessed, I had to use against that madman in the bamboo grove."

Satisfied with the complexity of this answer the Hachiman samurai respectfully bowed his thanks.

"Now" said the old master, "Your part of the bargain, answer me this –"

The Hachiman samurai looked full into the old eyes, he waited for the question.

"What is your name?"

The samurai breathed in deeply – honour demanded an answer, and a truthful one at that, there could be no hiding from this matter.

"My name is Kuroda Ichitaro of the Oka clan. My father was the samurai Kuroda Saburo. We trace back five generations in the loyal service of the Oka clan. I am seeking the chamberlain Miyake Rintaro, who by foul deception, murdered my lord."

CHAPTER SEVEN

ESCAPE

In the realm of the ninja, the master Tada made his decision.

"Send attack group four to the area and complete the task."

"Complete" was the slang for assassination – it held no mystery. The task would be completed in the most efficient manner, and silently. The ninja rarely resorted to open murder but preferred, as was their art, to work their skill in darkness. With their knowledge of poisons, a task could be

Furizue

Castle

completed over a period of time so that the unfortunate victim would seem to fade away – captured by demons as it were.

Many a lord in his fine castle had met his end this way – even the most knowledgeable physician could not tell where the hand of the ninja was at work. Masters of disguise, a ninja could infiltrate a castle as a servant, perform his daily tasks and remain, to act as "a sleeping tiger" – a dormant spy. The Tomokatsu Ryu had many such "sleeping tigers" – some slept for many years, until they were awoken to perform their duty.

The master Tada thought for a moment as he considered the strength of the samurai with the Hachiman tattoo.

"Send attack group five to back up the action."

This was the group led by the young Kichibei, it might prove useful to have his unconventional spirit.

The master Tada was stopped by the sound of running

in the corridor outside. The sound echoed around the rough stone room. It grew louder and louder, then a ninja guard burst into the room. Disregarding the sanctity of the two inquisitors, the guard addressed himself to the master Tada.

Tada looked sternly at the man.

"What is the meaning of this intrusion?"

His voice boomed in the tiny room – the inquisitors

The sleeping tiger wakes

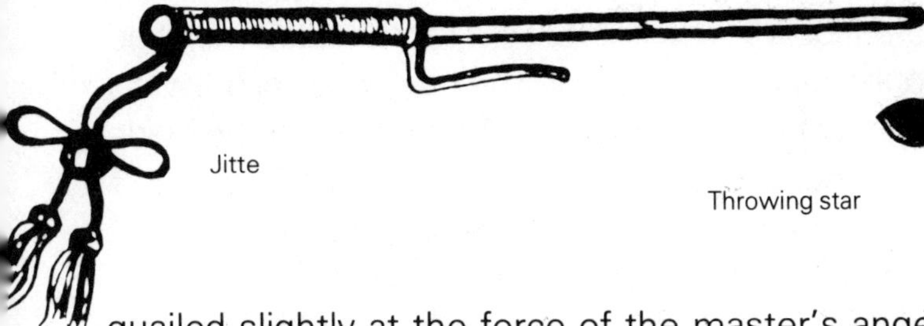

Jitte

Throwing star

quailed slightly at the force of the master's anger.

"Master! Important news from surveillance team three. The Hachiman samurai has disappeared."

"What!" shouted Tada, the possibility of the loss of a fee, flashed through his mind.

"Explain!"

"Surveillance team three, made all precautions after the duel and the visit to the old swordsmith. We know that he entered a bamboo grove on the high road, but he did not leave by this same road."

"What evidence?" asked Tada.

His prey had escaped his net, the loss of face for the Tomokatsu Ryu was great. If his client should find out and decide to use another ninja clan, the effects could be devastating. Loyalty to the clan was one thing, but in the face of failure, the solidarity of its members would be strained. A ninja who loses faith in the clan is open to bribery and even defection. It had happened many times before, to other clans and they had perished, eaten from within.

"What evidence?" Tada's voice again boomed out.

"One dead in the bamboo grove."

"Method of death?" Tada's voice was clipped.

"Massive damage to the spinal column, evidence of severe nervous spasm to the right forearm and centre of chest."

"Sword wounds?"

"None at all"

"Status of dead one?" demanded Tada.

"Dressed as a samurai, clothes too big, hair wrong, hakama tied incorrectly, scabbard mouth sliced."

This last fact was the final proof that the dead man had been masquerading as a smaurai. The true samurai drew his sword smoothly from its scabbard. Any cuts from the blade in the soft wooden heart of the laquered scabbard was a stain on the skill and the honour of a samurai.

"So – not a samurai" Tada stated.

"No master, we suspect a farmer's son, chancing his luck."

"Hmm" pondered Tada. "This is not our man's work, he would use the sword, his skill is not that perfect."

"What tracks?"

"Three pairs master – the dead one's, an old man and our samurai."

"So – the older man is the one" mused Tada, his face already dark, darkened further. He knew of the reputation of "the wandering one", as villagers called him. Tada knew he was an invincible warrior who had laid his weapons to rest and drawn away from the world, moving around in the mountains to avoid contact with human beings. Some even said he had become a tengu, a legendary figure who inhabited the forests. In legend they were masters of swordsmanship, capable even of flying. But the fact was that he was an old samurai who had some skill and wished to await his end in seclusion, studying the ways of nature.

"So," said Tada, "Our man has taken up with the old man in the mountains. It is not as bad as I had thought, he only has a short time. Saturate the area, cover all villages, all roads and passes.It is only a matter of time. Our samurai will emerge. He must, for his business is unfinished."

"Yes master" said the guard.

Lock picks

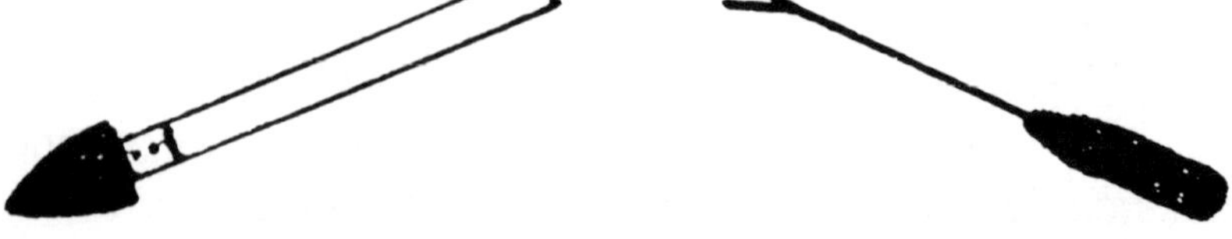

He turned and left. His footsteps, echoed back up the corridor, until the silence returned. Tada gazed blankly at the wall, his face impassive, but his mind buzzing with a thousand thoughts, plans and counter-plans, subterfuge and betrayal.

The inquisitor Kikushujo cleared his throat to speak.

"Silence!" commanded Tada, "I must make a decision this day which may effect the very lineage of the Tomokatsu Ryu!"

CHAPTER EIGHT

SPIRAL OF DEATH

"Kuroda Ichitaro, of the Oka clan." The old man, master of the 'spirit of the wind', spoke in a soft voice.

"Kuroda Ichitaro, " he repeated, all the time gazing into the eyes of the samurai, now his pupil, albeit for a short time.

With a movement so fast that it seemed to blur, the old man threw the tea bowl straight at Kuroda's face. Kuroda raised his hand and gently caught the bowl, he laid it softly by his side.

"Good, very good, you learn fast, Kuroda Ichitaro. But you must study deeper, for the true heart of the wind spirit is to freeze the mind for an instant."

"Freeze the mind?" asked Kuroda, puzzled.

"You must know the desires of your opponent's heart before they manifest themselves in his mind and he acts upon them. You must have the power to cut an opponent down even as the desire forms in his heart to kill you. Step to one side as the archer levels his bow."

"How can this come about? I have fought many men in single combat – men of equal, and I truly believe, superior ability, yet I have lived this long."

"You have been lucky," replied the old man.

"Lucky?" queried Kuroda.

Ninja

The spirit of the wind

"Yes, you rely on tricks and have been fortunate that Kwannon has bestowed her mercy upon you,"

Kuroda was silent, the depth and truth of the old man's words chilled him to the very marrow of his bones.

"So," continued the old man," you must surely meet an opponent who has a trick which is superior to yours. Luck eventually runs out. The truth of the spirit of the wind is that it relies upon nothing."

"Nothing?"

"Nothing, for where does the wind come from and where does it go? The principles which I have taught you are but a small part of the great truth which can reveal itself to you. I have only just begun to realise the extent of the teaching. Sword and spear are not ends in themselves, only a beginning. When the beginning becomes an end in itself, the true way is lost. I have seen skillful men who devoted their lives to the sword and in the end, the sword stole their souls away."

Kuroda was struck dumb at the enormity of the old man's teaching. He appreciated a small part of it, but much of what he said seemed incomprehensible. But the seed had been planted within Kuroda's heart and in the natural course, the realisation of its truth would flower.

The old man paused in his discourse as if sensing the air. He became sad, with a detached note in his voice, he said, "It must be."

Kuroda did not understand this last statement. As he began to speak, the old man leapt up in the air, over Kuroda's head. Landing softly on the floor behind him, gently, but swiftly removing the long spear from its rack, the old man whirled it once and then thrust the spear through the thatched straw roof. The spear found its mark. There was a piercing scream from above and the spear spun in decreasing arcs, pinned in its quarry.

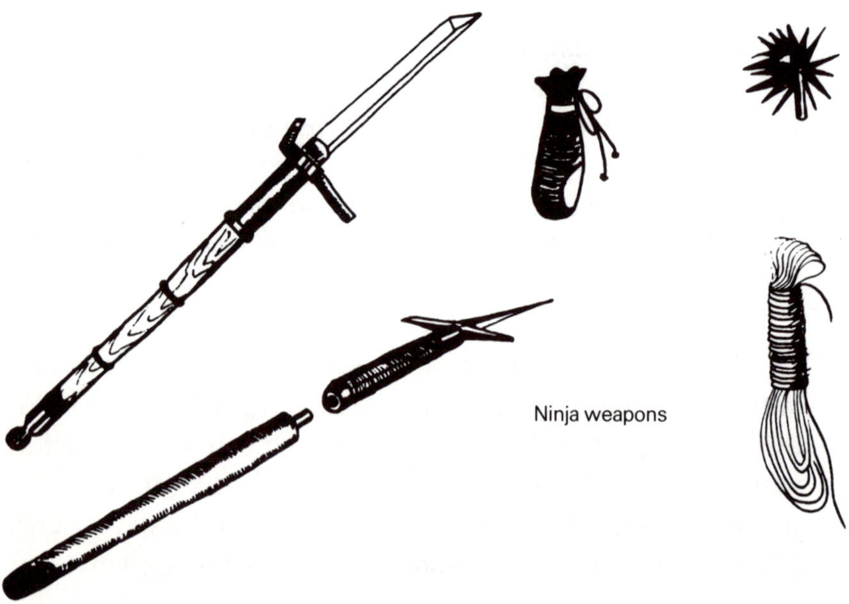

Ninja weapons

Ninja climbing rope

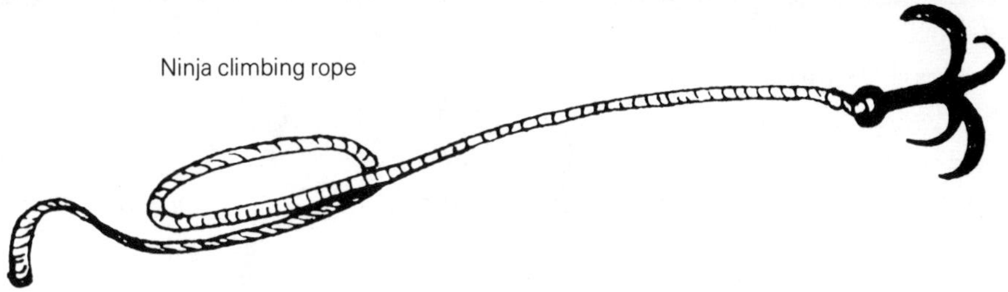

As Kuroda reacted to this with faster reactions than normal men, the old man was faster. He had taken down the long-bladed naginata halberd and dashed out of the hut.

"Observe the spirit of the wind!" he called behind him as he rushed into the clearing.

Agile as a cat he bounded from one side to another, never running in a straight path. His halberd sliced in figure of eight patterns as a hail of arrows was unleashed towards him. The arrows split and fell harmlessly to the ground. Out of the trees a black clad figure dropped silently. The halberd hissed as it met its mark, cutting the ninja from surveillance team three in half at the waist.

Kuroda watched, knowing that he must not intervene, for this was his best lesson in "the spirit of the wind." The spear, which lately, the old man had thrust through the roof, fell to the ground. Kuroda jumped slightly, the ninja who had been its victim, tumbled to the ground, falling heavily. Kuroda continued to watch from the darkness of the hut.

Another ninja leapt up at the old man, whirling the ten thousand power chain. As the chain slashed towards the old man, he reversed his grip and as the chain was caught with the butt end of the naginata, it snaked around the shaft. The old man pulled slightly as the chain took hold, the ninja's balance was broken as he fell forward, the naginata blade cut him from left shoulder to right hip.

The old man dropped the naginata and walked calmly and slowly forward. Two ninja leapt towards him, their straight bladed swords flashing in the dark forest as they made for their target. Suddenly, the old man was not there, he had moved rapidly: the ninja cut each other dead.

Ninja climbing pole

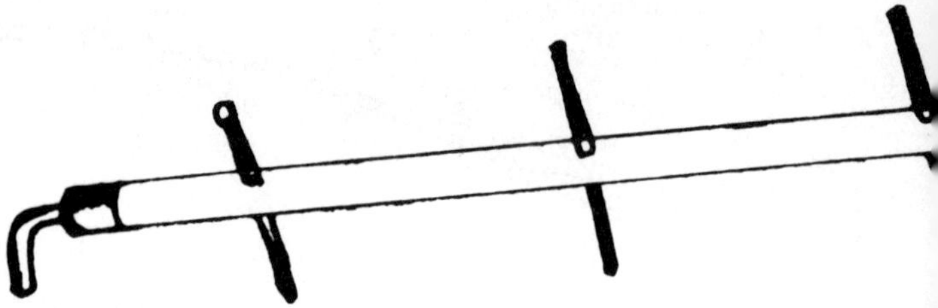

Kuroda gazed on enthralled. The very secrets of the wind spirit were revealing themselves to him through the old master's technique. As the two ninja cut each other, Kuroda realised the meaning of the master's words "freeze the mind". Like some kind of hypnosis, the master had made the ninja think he was still where he was not.

One last ninja, possibly the most formidable, for this was the surveillance team leader, stepped forward. The old man stood still as the ninja reached into his kimono and took a throwing star. The eight-pointed razor flew. The old man did not move, surely he must be struck. But the inexplicable happened, the star curved in its arc. Was this magic, or was even Kuroda hypnotised? The aura from the old man was electrifying, Kuroda's grasp of the sixth sense, puny though it was compared to the force he was experiencing, warned him that something decisive was about to occur.

There stood the old man, unarmed as he had been in the bamboo grove. There stood the ninja fully armed. What Kuroda had witnessed in the bamboo grove was elementary compared to what was about to happen here. The old man was doing this intentionally, extending the duel, as a graduation lesson for Kuroda. The ultimate lesson a master can give, one in the very face of death.

The ninja reached over his right shoulder and drew his sword. He adopted a strong defensive posture and waited. This ninja was good, very good. Kuroda recognised the rudiments of the ninja's style – it had some of the points of the reverse dragonfly style of the warriors of Shimazu Han. But there were subtle differences.

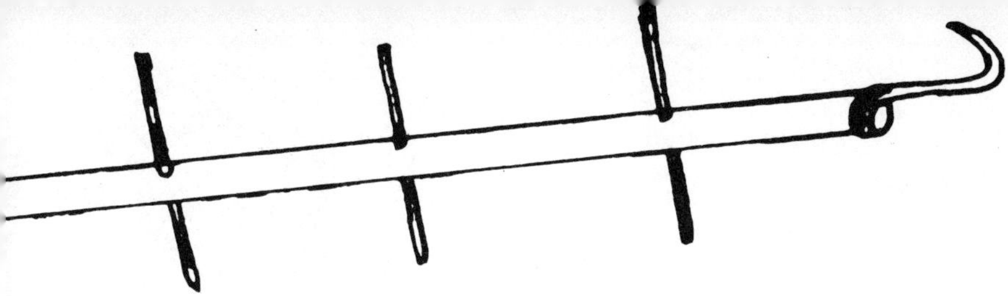

The old man then did the unexpected, he sat down, crossed one leg over the other and waited. The ninja circled him, his sword weaving in the reverse dragonfly pattern, creating neither beginning nor end to a technique. The old man remained as he was, staring in front of him. The ninja circled until he stood behind the master. Then the ninja attacked. Fearing the end, Kuroda rushed out to engage the ninja, then the impossible happened. As the ninja sword made for the old man's head, he raised his hands in the air, clapping them together as the blade whistled down. There was a sharp, metallic crack as the sword blade was shattered by the old hands.

The ninja, his balance now broken, toppled forward, only to be hoisted by the old man and flipped to his feet. He flew through the air and then thudded to the ground – no straw palliases to break his return to earth. His skull crushed and his back was broken.

The air became quiet again, gently picking up his naginata, the old man walked back to the hut, scarcely out of breath.

"Join me for some tea", he said to the awestruck Kuroda.

CHAPTER NINE

SHINO

In the Palace of Pleasure are a thousand delights. Those who choose the path of the floating world, would shun the light of day, living only for the fleeting ecstacy of a moment's pleasure.

Those whose life was the service of these pleasures, lived in the perpetual dream, where all is beauty, all is pleasure – until age scarred their faces and the world of the senses floated away, leaving them alone.

The servants of the Kanda house were usually young country girls. Virgins sold by their families, for a girl had no merit, unlike a son, better therefore to make some money from her at least.

So the young virgins entered the service, working the skills of their bodies to the highest bidder, to samurai, merchants and sometimes priests. Of all the girls who served their lives away at the Kanda house, where Madam Kiku ruled with the absolute power of one who has escaped the natural fate of her profession – only Shino personally chose her clients.

She was expensive, no one knew where she came from, what her history was or what was her hold over Madam Kiku. Some of the girls gossiped that she must be Kiku's daughter. But this was just gossip, the truth was far stranger, for the Madam Kiku feared the slender Shino.

Shino's clothes were of the finest silk, her room better furnished than even Madam Kiku's personal apartment. The edging to the tatami matting covering the floor of her room was of the highest quality brocade. The cups from which she served warm sake to her clients was of superb black laquer,

Shino

with tiny tombo dragonflies in red laquer. And her laundry was done by her own maid servant. The girls would have loved to have gleaned Shino's secrets from this source, but the girl was a deaf mute, with whom Shino communicated in delicate finger signs.

This night was no different, Shino's room had been prepared by her servant. A small portable hibachi brazier, fitted cleverly in a strangely formed piece of drift wood. On the glowing charcoal was an iron pan filled with water in which nestled several ceramic bottles of gently warming sake – enough to make even the most nervous client mellow – and talkative.

The delicately painted fusuma screen door was slid open by the Madam Kiku. In her late forties, she wore a kimono of midnight blue, with her namesake flowers, Kiku, chrysanthemums, embroidered in rich, nishiki brocade. Tied tightly around her waist was the twelve inch wide obi sash in watered orange silk. Her face was powdered white in the manner of fine ladies and her teeth were laquered black. She complimented the prospective client and the talk was titillatingly suggestive. Her tongue darted between her teeth in the classic manner of the women of the floating world.

"Please enjoy the pleasures of the Kanda house, there are books to help your mood."

She gestured to a small laquer case containing the shunga, pornographic "pillow books," profusely illustrated and drawn in the finest detail.

"There is warm sake to comfort your spirit. The lady Shino, (her girls were always referred to as 'lady') will be with you presently."

She pursed her lips, the tongue darted, "Enjoy yourself."

She slid the fusuma door shut.

The client was a minor official of a visiting lord. He had heard of Shino's charms and was most pleased that she had agreed to be his partner for the evening. He sat down and

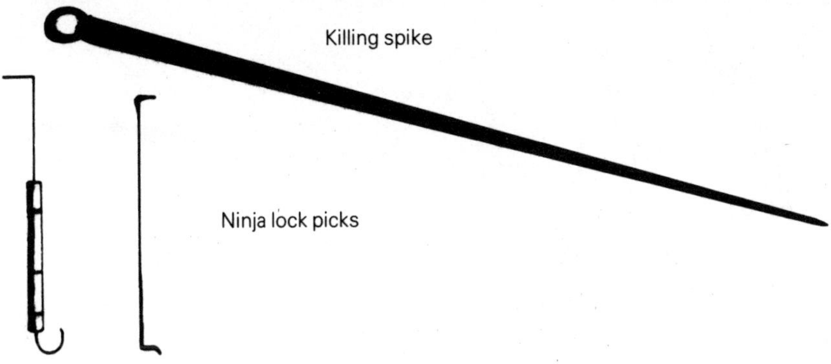

poured himself a drink. He drank the liquid, savouring its warmth. Turning to the elegant case containing the shunga, he drew one out, unfolded it and began to study the tiny drawings.

With a gentle swish, the fusuma opened and closed. Startled, the official looked up. There, framed by the elegant doorway, stood the lady Shino. She was far more beautiful than he had imagined. Dressed in a purple silk kimono with a flame red silk obi sash, its huge knot tied in the front, in the manner of the classical courtesans of the Heian court. She gestured for the man not to move, he remained transfixed by her beauty.

With a smooth movement she turned on the spot. Her back towards him, she unfastened the clip holding her hair. It cascaded down, almost reaching the floor, swaying gently like a long black curtain.

The man caught his breath as she turned her head and looked over her shoulder at him. At the same time, the red obi fell to the floor and her kimono billowed around her. She fixed the man with her dark eyes, framed by the shimmering curtain of hair.

The man shuddered.

"You are beautiful."

Shino drew her hand to her mouth, one delicate finger extended.

"Do not speak", she said softly. "Prepare yourself for an ecstasy of pleasure."

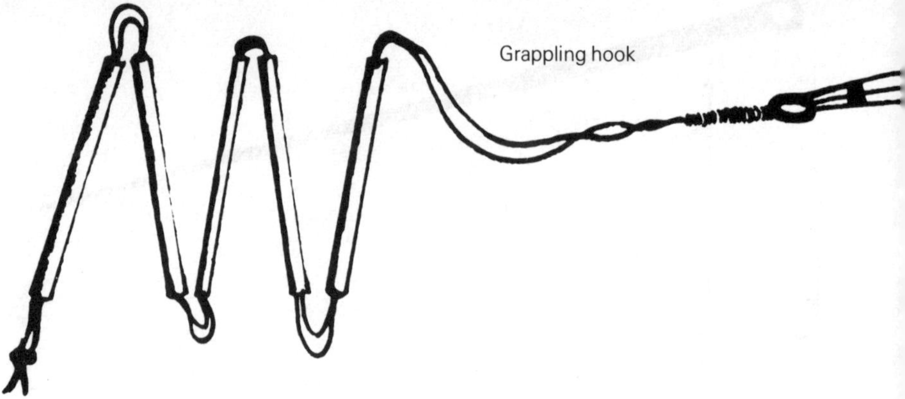

Grappling hook

The man looked on – still with her back towards him she slowly let the kimono slide from her shoulders. It slipped down her back, causing her hair to ripple in dark, gleaming streaks. It slid over the milky paleness of her skin and the smooth curve of her back until it stopped at the soft roundness of her behind. She turned slightly, revealing the tiny breasts with their pink centres standing erect in the soft light of the room that was her palace of pleasure, her domain of the senses.

Still holding the kimono like a cloak, she turned and walked towards him. Beads of sweat formed on his brow as he saw the extent of her naked beauty. She stood close to him and then slowly sat down, drawing the kimono over them both. The sake and the shunga were forgotten in the ecstasy of the moment.

From the distance, in the real world, came the haunting sound of a shaku hachi flute as it played a soulful four note repetition, again and again.

Throwing block

In the house of the Kanda prostitutes a sleeping tiger awoke. At the peak of his excitement the man did not feel Shino's tiny hand close around his ear. There was a sharp click and a gurgle as his life slipped away, ended by the technique of simultaneous nerve shock. To a physician it would appear that the excitement of the moment had been too great for his heart to bear. "A fine way to go" the physician would probably say.

No one would question the fact that the girl had disappeared, naturally a reputation for killing clients; even in such an enjoyable situation, would not be good for business.

What no one, save for Madam Kiku, knew, was that Shino was a Kunoichi, a female ninja of the Tomokatsu Ryu. Madam Kiku also knew that she would never betray this secret, she was fully aware of the extent of ninja vengeance.

Shino would have been 'retired to the country' to recover, as far as her 'regulars' from whom she obtained much of her information for the intelligence group, were concerned. These regulars found Shino's conversation stimulated their minds as well as their bodies. Trying to impress her with their importance, they happily gave away secrets of their lords. This was sifted and stored away for future use.

The go code for murder, to which Shino had responded without second thought, had been from the ninja Chubei who had journeyed to Kyoto under the express order of the Master Tada.

Silently Shino dressed in her travelling clothes and left unobserved. The Madam Kiku would have to think quickly when the dead man was discovered and Shino's absence noted. But one does not become the madam of a house such as the Kanda without being able to think quickly in extreme situations.

On the road north out of Kyoto, no one noticed the boy and the blind man as they made their way slowly, but surely to the Master Tada.

CHAPTER TEN

MEMORIAL OF FATE

The warmth of the tea was comforting, the Hachiman samurai, Kuroda Ichitaro, looked at the old master of the spirit of the wind.

"You must leave this place?"

The old master looked at Kuroda and summoning all the wisdom of his age and skill, answered,

"One place is as good as another, nature is boundless. You have been my pupil for so short a time, but this," he gestured towards the battleground of fallen ninja, "this was your graduation. I have shown you the very heart of the spirit of the wind – make what use of it you can."

"Others may follow you" said Kuroda, referring to the ninja.

The old man looked surprised. "Do you not realise that it is you, whom they seek?"

Kuroda shivered slightly, "But why? I am searching for the chamberlain, Miyake Rintaro – because of his action no clan will knowingly harbour him, and he certainly could not

One cut!

Calm fury

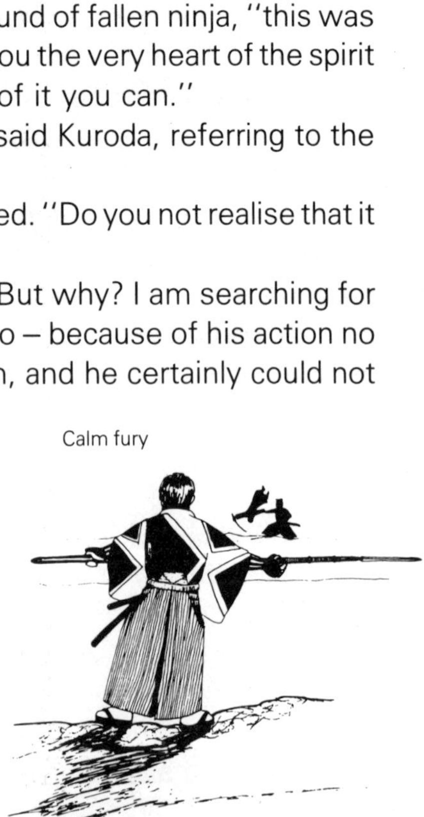

The Warrior

Ninja halberd

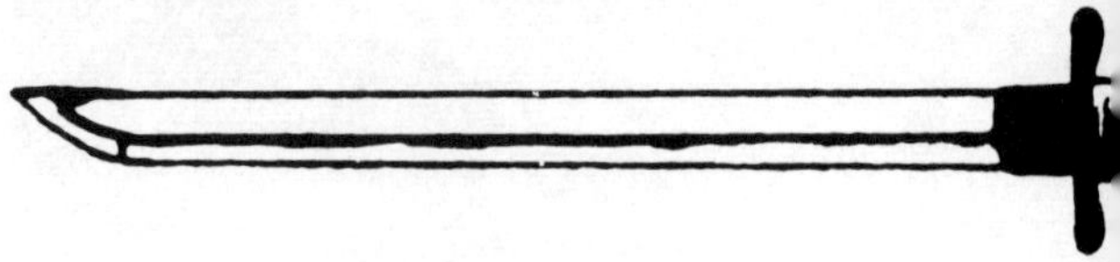

Ninja climbing frame

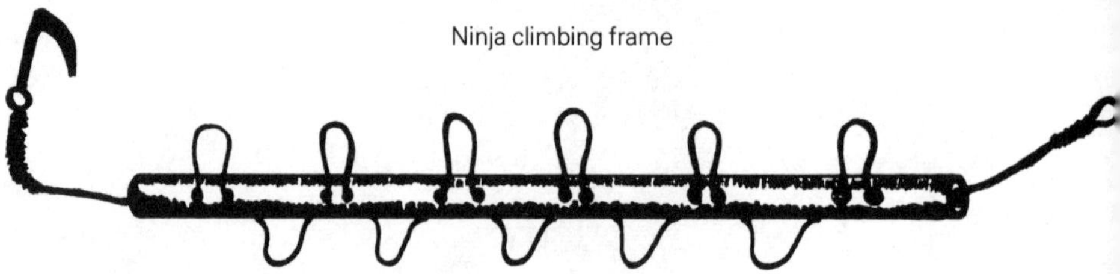

pay for ninja to stop me.''

''Calm your mind'' replied the old man, ''do not search for the answer, let it find you.''

Kuroda sat in the posture of meditation, that was the core of the spirit of the wind. He calmed his mind. He sat without moving. Ten minutes, an hour passed. A blinding whiteness in his mind, within which the answer formed. The internal art of the spirit of the wind bordered on the realms of the occult, powers which few true men possessed, but which many false ones pretended to have.

Slowly events and reasons fitted together in Kuroda's mind, like one of the intricate wooden puzzles for which the toymakers of Osaka are famous.

Kuroda saw the entire scene in brief flashes, observed firstly in random order, then gradually assuming a logical pattern.

He was back at the village where the duel had taken place. The samurai he had killed was also there, in the inn with his travelling companions. They all bore the same family crest, save one, the travelling priest. The group had been engaged in earnest conversation, the priest listening intently.

Kuroda's mind went blank, he calmed himself again . . .

Now he was high up in a tree outside the swordsmith's hut, looking down upon himself as he bathed the newly cauterized wound in his chest, he watched himself turn to reveal the Hachiman tattoo.

Again his mind clouded, slowly it cleared once more: he saw a field, recognised it as the field where the duel had been fought. But it was bathed in a half-light, like that just before the dawn, he saw figures and then heard voices.

"Why challenge the samurai at the inn to fight?" asked one.

"I wish to test his skill," came the reply.

"But you may die" objected a third.

"We all die!" the voice replied as the sun broke the horizon. Kuroda saw in his mind's eye that this voice belonged to the samurai he had fought and killed.

"And if you are killed, we shall owe a debt of honour to our lord for letting this happen."

"I absolve you of all blame – take this note, it will explain everything."

Then came a fourth voice, it was that of the priest.

"My master Tada has instructed me to act for you in all matters. Our retainer is great indeed. If you die, we will regard it as our debt and will avenge you".

"If you must," said the samurai.

"But he did not give his name", said one.

"We will find him, name or not," replied the priest.

"Leave me – for this work only I can accomplish – I must know who is better."

Kuroda's mind again became blank, this time it did not clear and he slumped forward.

The master of the spirit of the wind gently cushioned his head.

"Too great a power, too soon", he thought, "but he will learn to control the mind search."

The great secret of the spirit of the wind, the 'occult' mind search, was indeed a high level. It risked the very sanity of those who employed it. But the old man was not unduly worried, his pupil was strong and to have lived to such an age – lucky. Would that luck last?

The old man drifted off into his own mind search, but being adept at its use, stopped short before the dangerous zone, unlike Kuroda.

Kuroda stirred then sat bolt upright. The old master looked at him.

"You have seen through the veil?"

"Yes".

"Then act on that knowledge – do not often use the secret I have shown you, for it can split the line between reality and the high level. You may one day remain on the high level, which is as good as death," he warned.

Kuroda did not answer but listened very carefully. Still reeling from the shock of his vision, he struggled to catch all that the master said, for he knew that they must soon journey along different paths.

CHAPTER ELEVEN

MORE TEA

The flea crawled from the man's hairline and made its way down to the warmth of the shabby kimono – the man scratched, finding the flea, he crushed it between thumb and forefinger.

"More sake!" came a shout.

The man absently wiped the remains of the flea between the folds of his kimono. He bent over the large cauldron hanging over the fire. It hung suspended by a hook bound to a large beam of timber. The whole contraption swayed slightly.

He lifted the lid on the cauldron, burning his hand. He spat out an oath in the local dialect, then pulled a rough stone jar out of the bubbling water by the hemp rope around its neck.

With the bottle swinging at his side, he slouched over to the table where two figures were bent over their business. The innkeeper put the bottle down on the table with a thud.

"More sake – more money."

A small coin was thrown on the table, the innkeeper snatched it up and put it to his mouth. He bared his teeth, black stumps most of them, but two good ones still remained, his coin testers as he called them. The coin testers closed upon the coin, satisfied he turned and walked back to his perch by the fire.

The interior of what could be called an inn, was dingy, the beams smoke-blackened and the floor rough compacted earth. In the rainy season it became a mire and customers were relegated to low wooden platforms. These served as a sleeping area for those who could pay the meagre sum to

More tea

stay the night, or were too drunk to be thrown out. The place contained about twenty people, all men. The innkeeper dreamed about being able to afford some girls, but the houses in the city snapped up the choicest fruits. Anyway, keep girls and you have to feed them. His clients were more interested in spending their money on drink, girls were a luxury. The innkeeper continued in his thoughts of big-hipped girls on whom he could ride away the nights.

The rough wooden door opened and closed with a crash, breaking into his erotic reverie. The newcomer was slightly built, aged about fifty – a samurai. His swords were covered with dark blue dyed cloth travelling covers. His clothes were sober and mud spattered from his journey. Seeing an empty space, away from the crowd, he crossed to it. Drawing his long sword, in its travelling cover, from his sash he sat down, placing the sword at his left side.

"Samurai are always trouble", thought the inn-keeper,"better not invite trouble to your house." The inn-keeper walked over to the seated figure.

"Yes," he quickly added, "Sir".

"Food" said the newcomer.

"And sake?" asked the innkeeper.

"And tea!" the samurai replied.

At a nearby table two roughs were in the depths of sake, one of the men laughed when he heard the request for tea. The newcomer was none other than the chamberlain, Miyake Rintaro – on the run from the avenging Kuroda. Miyake was forced to use these lowly inns, for the chance of being discovered here was less than at a house more suited to his status.

The innkeeper returned with the boiled wheat and the tea. Miyake began to eat. He had not eaten for three days, regardless of his behaviour and present situation, he was still a samurai by birth and old habits die hard. Thus, he ate the wheat as though he had last eaten only a few minutes before. He poured some tea and began to drink. His thirst was great and the pot was soon emptied.

"Hey innkeeper," the innkeeper looked across.

"Sir?"

"More tea!" said Miyake.

"More tea" echoed the two roughs, "More tea!" they giggled wildly. Miyake stood up, taking his long sword he carefully unwrapped the travelling cloth. He folded the cloth exactly and placed it in the folds of his kimono. The inn fell silent, no one moved.

Miyake held the sword lightly by the scabbard, in his left hand. The roughs, too drunk to notice the tension in the

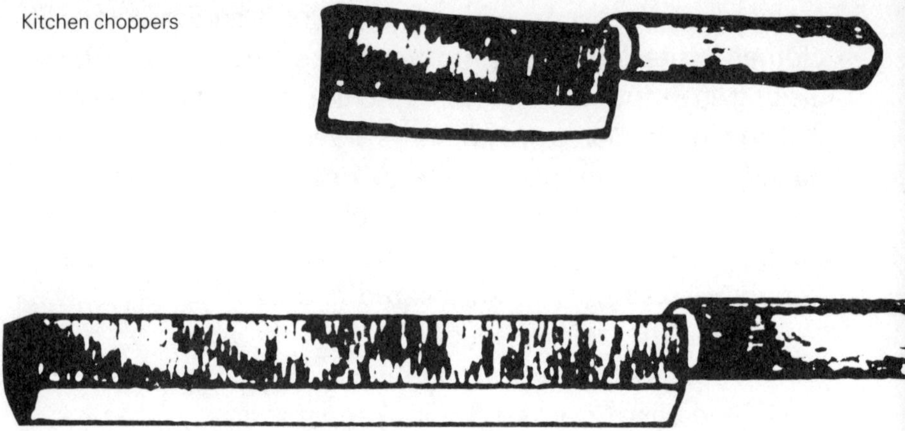

Kitchen choppers

escalating situation, continued in their ridicule. "More tea!" said one, pouring sake into his partner's cup. "More tea!" said the other, he belched and laughed crudely.

The innkeeper had disappeared behind the low wall which housed the sacks of wheat and rice. "Oh no, not again", he moaned to himself as he awaited the outcome.

The pair of roughs grew louder and louder in their ridicule. Miyake walked over and sat down next to them. They were silenced by this, but only for a moment. As they started off again, Miyake softly spoke, "Why do you want to die?"

"Eh?" muttered one. He was the bigger of the two, a labourer by trade, strong as an ox, with about as much brain.

His friend sobered up as quickly as if he'd been thrown into an icy stream. He frantically looked for an escape, but there was none.

The big ox stared dully at Miyake. He laughed and looked at his friend. "More tea!" he giggled, but there was no answering snigger; his friend had gone white.

"Why do you want to die?" Miyake asked again.

"I, I don't want to die" stuttered the ox stupidly.

"Then better have more sake, eh?" said Miyake. "Innkeeper!"

A head popped up from behind the low wall, "Sir?"

"More sake for my companions, all they can drink."

The innkeeper stood up and drew two of the rough stone jars from the cauldron. He walked over to Miyake and the two louts. This time he made no mention of money, he was happy that his head still sat upon his shoulders, he intended to keep it that way.

Miyake poured a stiff measure for each of the two men. "Drink", he said. They drank, he refilled their cups and they drank again.

The other occupants of the inn started to drink and talk and the potential danger was forgotten as the sake clouded both judgement and memory.

The two jars became four, then six. The two roughs had always dreamed of drinking like this, now their dreams had become reality.

"Where you come from?" slurred the big ox.

"There", Miyake answered.

"Where you going?"

Miyake pointed in the opposite direction.

"There!"

This seemed to satisfy the ox and he drained his sake cup.

The midnight hour had passed. Most of the inn had cleared, some were huddled on the wooden platform where they snored loudly and broke wind in the blissful ignorance of their alcoholic stupor.

The innkeeper lightly dozed, waiting for Miyake and the two roughs to either fall asleep, leave, or kill each other. He had ceased caring, he drifted back to his fantasies of the broad-hipped girls of his dreams.

Miyake poured the sake, the big ox was still going

strong. His companion lifted his cup to his lips, missed and slumped forward, oblivious in his sake-sodden sleep. The big ox roared out his crude laugh.

Miyake began to probe, he knew the way of these louts – more information could be gleaned from their silences than from their words.

"Seen any samurai around?"

The ox picked up his cup and emptied it.

"Nah! Just you. More tea!" he giggled stupidly.

Miyake refilled his cup.

"Any strangers?"

"Nah, same old faces."

Any temples?"

"Yeh, up on the north road, crazy men!"

The big ox closed his eyes and began to snore.

Miyake rose and threw some coins at the innkeeper – who, waking in an instant, caught them.

"Thank you sir" he shouted, to the open doorway.

Miyake trudged up the north road out of town.

The dark warrior

CHAPTER TWELVE

THE WAY OF THE WORLD

The blind man and the boy walked down the road into familiar territory. As was ninja practice – the outward signs masked the inner truth. The blind man could see and the boy was a girl. The shakuhachi player of the go code which awoke the sleeping tiger, was disguised as the blind man, and the young boy was no other than the lady Shino, courtesan and Kunoichi ninja. Even dressed as a boy, her long black hair rolled up in a simple rain hat, she was stunningly beautiful. Whenever she decided to retire or was retired from active service, there would be no shortage of ninja men who would take her for a wife. Regardless of what she had been in her life outside the ninja stronghold; within the safety of the Tomokatsu Ryu all exterior duties were forgotten. Thus the assassin was absolved from his actions by the ninja code – called Zankanjo – absolution from responsibility for their actions. So, although Shino sold "spring" in the Palace of the Dragon King, as her trade and her work place were known, she was absolved from any moral stigma upon her return.

Once she reached the ninja stronghold, the master Tada was to brief her for her next mission – this would involve her with Kuroda, the samurai with the Hachiman tattoo.

Kuroda was also on the road again, in search of the chamberlain Miyake Rintaro, but he was a man now wiser in two respects. Firstly in the seeds of the knowledge beyond knowing, sight beyond seeing and skill beyond technique, that was the spirit of the wind. Secondly he was now aware that he was a hunted man. No one could be trusted and the

The Abbot Sochin

obvious could not be trusted as such. The ninja of the Tomokatsu Ryu held a debt of obligation to find him and see him dead.

The master of the spirit of the wind looked around his forest glade, at the place which was once a peaceful home, now transformed into a battlefield. It was time to move on, to find another place and await the end in quiet contemplation. He gathered only the essentials for his journey. His tea kettle and utensils and the weapons which he was loath to leave. They were like his children and he knew them well, though in technique far beyond them, he could not let them go, it was his weakness. So with his furoshiki wrapping cloth containing his possessions in one hand, his long and short swords thrust in his sash and his spears and naginata resting on his shoulder, he left his home, quietly and without turning back.

The chamberlain Miyake Rintaro had found the north road and was making his way to the Shoto-ji temple, where he hoped he would find a haven. A refuge for a short time before the confrontation with Kuroda – whom he knew would not cease searching until he had found him and seen him dead.

In the wide world, the affairs of individuals are but a pile of dust in the face of the storm. For events were brewing in the land which would draw the fates of Kuroda, Miyake and the Tomokatsu Ryu to a far stranger conclusion than could be dreamed of.

To the west, a mighty army was massing, under the command of the general Ieyasu of the Tokugawa family.. To the east formed the forces of the Toyotomi family under the command of the general Ishida Mitsunori. Before the month's end, they would meet.

The narrow road to the deep north inclined ever upwards. Miyake trudged on – in his heart he felt as one of the dead, for he knew that Kuroda could never understand the reasons for him killing his lord. Kuroda was a yojimbo samurai, his whole life was service, he expected nothing more than to save his lord in life and to join him in death. Miyake knew that only the fact of his lord's murder had stayed Kuroda's hand from committing seppuku – slashing his abdomen with his short sword and joining his lord – the burden hardest to bear. Miyake also knew that Kuroda was a skilful swordsman, who knew many tricks and that he did not stand a chance – so he must seek rest, make his peace with his ancestors and await death.

The long road, old and well-trodden by the footsteps of the faithful drew to its end. Miyake stood before the gateway of the Shoto-ji temple. Once, it had been a vast monastery, housing over five thousand monks – warrior monks, yama bushi, skilled in the sword and spear. But two hundred and fifty years before, a vast army had laid siege to the monastery and burned it to the ground. Out of the ashes had grown the building before which Miyake now stood. It was small and compact, housing one hundred or so monks, under the leadership of the abbot Sochin – the silent one. In the depths of the fireproof Kura warehouse he held the secret scrolls of the Yama bushi, perhaps one day they would rise again, when the country needed them.

Miyake picked up the short hardwood staff from its niche in the outside wall of the gateway. With this he struck the bell – its ringing echoed, a moment passed and the small door within the gateway opened. Facing him was a young monk, about 17 years of age, his shaven head shone slightly as he bowed forward.

"Sir?" said the monk.

"I seek rest" said Miyake.

"Please enter and await my senior's decision."

Miyake bent as he entered the small doorway. Once inside he saw the large carved wooden Gods which stood on either side of the gateway – Nio, guardians, one to kill desire and one to kill the ego.

"Please sir," said the young monk, "weapons are for-

The great general

bidden beyond the gateway."

Obediently, Miyake removed both his swords and placed them in the long rack which stretched nearly to the ceiling – it was empty save for his two weapons.

"Please remove your shoes and leave them here."

Once again, Miyake obeyed, the significance of this action was that one stepped out of the world and into the realisation of one's inner self. The shoes symbolised the leaving behind of the reason for entering.

Following the young monk down the long wooden corridors, the planks creaked and sang as their feet fell upon them. Evening was fast approaching. The young monk showed Miyake to a small anteroom, he slid the shoji screen, which served as a window, to one side.

"Please wait."

Miyake entered and sat down, the young monk walked off to his seniors. The evening light slowly dimmed as Miyake gazed out on the garden. The garden was as deceptively simple as the swordsmith's had been. A revelation of the doctrine of self-realisation, a world in miniature. Miyake relaxed as the feelings of age and faith that the monastery held, flooded over him.

The footsteps returned. The young monk bowed.

"My Abbot Sochin will see you, please come with me."

Miyake rose and left the room – as they walked down yet another long corridor, bounded again on one side by garden. The deep sonorous chanting of the ancient sutras vibrated from the meditation hall. At regular intervals the chanting stopped and a bell or a drum was struck, then the chanting began again.

The young monk stopped before a raised doorway, he bowed and knocked. "Enter!" The young monk slid the screen door and, on his knees, walked forward into the presence of the Abbot Sochin. He bowed, this time his head touched the mat, he raised his hands, palms upwards, in the most respectful form of bow, which was reserved for the Abbot alone. Following the priest, Miyake bowed slightly, for he was still samurai.

"Be seated," said the Abbot Sochin, gesturing with the bamboo stick which he held in his right hand. Miyake sat formally, with his feet tucked under him – often referred to as seiza.

The young monk left, he slid the screen door shut. The room was bathed in a soft yellow light from a small lamp. The room was sparse, in the alcove was its only decoration – a hanging scroll, its base was a reserved brown brocade with a white paper panel in the centre. On this panel was a circle drawn roughly and the characters "great emptiness" written in the same rough ink brush style.

The Abbot Sochin, the silent one, sat in the full meditation posture of the hanka fusa; both feet crossed over both

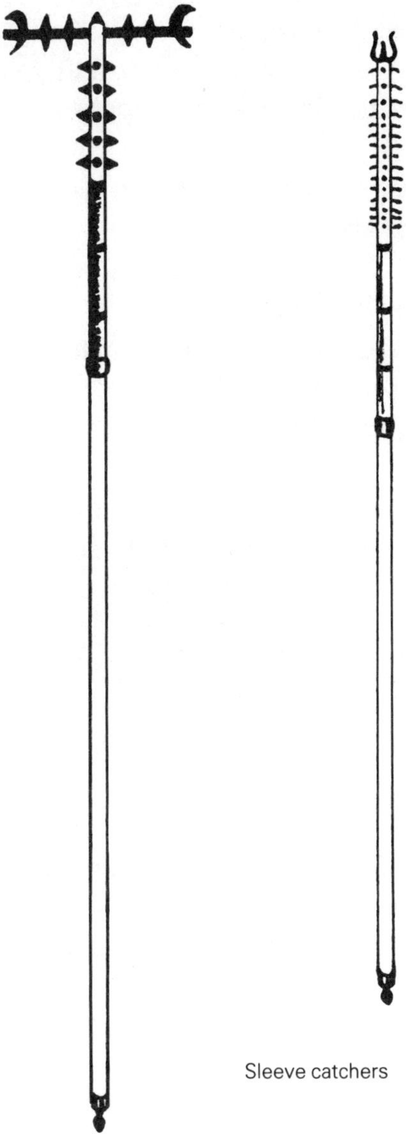

Sleeve catchers

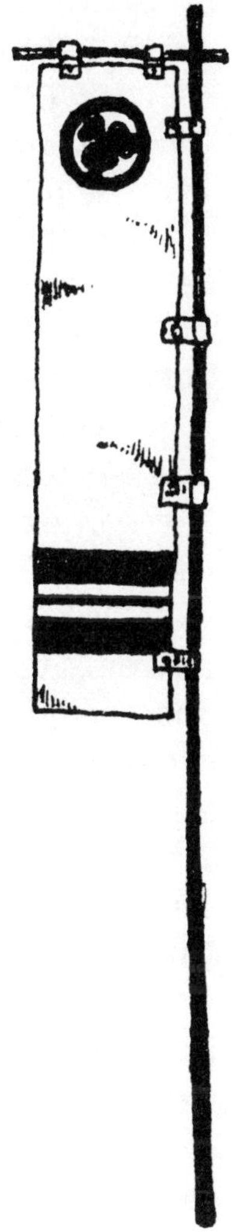

Samurai Banner

thighs. His clothes were simple black, no different in style or quality to those of the most lowly novice monk. Around his neck hung the black, bib-like kesa – the symbol of his devotion. Yet in these simple clothes, he appeared a giant, such was his composure and faith.

Miyake waited for the Abbot to speak, he waited and waited. It seemed like hours were passing – hours which were in reality only ten minutes.

Then the Abbot spoke. He spoke slowly, very softly, almost choosing each word and listening to it as he spoke it.

"What do you seek?"

"Forgive my impetuousness, but soon I should die."

"So must we all", said the Abbott.

"Please, you do not understand – I have committed a great crime and an avenger comes for my life."

"You will live for precisely the time, the universal truth has allotted you – no more and no less"

Miyake paused in his thoughts as the Abbott continued speaking –

"When we meditate, we are under the protection of the universal truth. If we were to meditate, thinking only of the moment of our deaths, it would be true to say that we are already dead."

Miyake, puzzled, finally said, "I don't understand."

At this, the Abbott roared with laughter and hitting Miyake hard on the head with the bamboo stick, said. "Go and meditate with my monks – ponder your words and my action."

The Abbott rang the small bell to signify the audience was at an end – behind Miyake, the door slid open.

"Visit me tomorrow", said the Abbot. Miyake bowed and left.

CHAPTER THIRTEEN

CONFRONTATION

Wary of all movements, Kuroda walked the road. He felt all eyes of the ninja upon him – but when he tried to use the spirit of the wind to locate them – they faded back into the shadows.

As Kuroda passed through the villages which sprang up along the road, he felt the stirrings of the great tumult that was to visit the land. Parties of Ashi-Garu – freelance foot soldiers were much in evidence, they were trying to decide whether to throw in their lot with the Toyotomi or Tokugawa mustermen.

With such a rag-tag collection of mercenaries in the countryside, one would have expected fighting and general civil disturbances. But that would be after the battle, when to the victor came the spoils, then the sport would be paid for – the pillage, murder and rape would occur all in the service of the victorious army. So the Ashi-Garu bided their time, carefully weighing the situation.

Kuroda strode on, brushing aside any requests to join either faction. Seeing his resolve, the Ashi-Garu gave him a wide berth. On the morning of the third day of his travels, after walking through the night, he came to a shabby village. "Time" he thought, "to rest." He saw the decrepit inn, Ashi-Garu all around it. They paid him no heed, choosing rather to play their dice and swear at each other. Some bathed in the filthy stream which bounded the inn.

They bathed in twos and threes, their comrades guarding their light chest armour and weapons on the banks. Their mood was expectant – anticipating a good fight and with luck, good sport as members of the victorious side. If they

Confrontation

found themselves on the losing side, then they could look forward to some exercise in fast running, but such was the mercenary way, some you lost and some you won.

Kuroda entered the inn. It too was crowded with Ashi-Garu, he found himself a place and ordered sake. He tossed a coin to the innkeeper, who, with so many Ashi-Garu around, was taking no chances. Samurai or not, he placed the coin to his two good teeth. "OK!" he said and put the stoneware flask down. He walked back to his perch, musing to himself. One week only his regulars and one crazy samurai who paid for two louts to get blind drunk. Now one week later, the inn was full to bursting with Ashi-Garu and samurai. Still, their money was good and providing he buried it in a safe place, it would be alright after the battle. The winning side would have plenty of money, better lay in more sake. Of course if the battle was too close he might get burned out, but he would see how his luck chose to go.

Kuroda felt Miyake was close by. But the nearness of the ninja and the Ashi-Garu forbade him trying to use the techniques taught him by the master of the spirit of the wind. But, no matter, Kuroda knew Miyake was near by, the desire to kill him was strong in his heart. He could almost taste the sweetness of his revenge.

"Going to buy me a drink?"

Kuroda looked up at a giant of a man, the same big ox whom Miyake had so recently plied with sake.

"Drink" said Kuroda, pushing the cup towards him.

A few short weeks before Kuroda would have cut him where he stood for such presumption, but he had begun to see things in less black and white terms.

The ox drank another cup of sake.

"You looking for someone?" he asked.

"Why do you ask?" queried Kuroda.

The man pointed unsteadily with a large stubby finger at the family crest of the oka clan which adorned Kuroda's kimono.

"Seen that before" he slurred.

"Oh yes" said Kuroda, pouring another cup of sake, "where?"

"Money" demanded the ox.

"Step outside, this place is too public for such talk."

The ox followed him out. Kuroda walked beside the stream, the inn and its bathing Ashi-Garu were a fair distance away, he sensed for ninja, they were there but were not close. Kuroda suddenly turned on the man, he stopped as quickly as his fuddled brain would allow.

"Now tell me, where did you see this?" he pointed to the crest.

"Money" persisted the ox.

"How much?" asked Kuroda.

"Lots" he muttered stupidly.

Kuroda drew his short sword in one rapid movement and pinned the man against a tree. The blade pricked into his neck and a tiny trickle of blood formed as the metal nicked the skin. Downstream the Ashi-Garu continued to bathe and play dice.

"Where?" Kuroda again asked.

"'Bout a week ago in the inn."

"Yes, then what?"

"Bought me an' my mate sake, we got good and drunk."

"Where did he go?"

"Dunno –"

The blade pushed in another quarter of an inch, the blood flowed faster.

"Think hard, for if you do not answer, I shall cut your head off."

The big ox's eyes widened, the urgency of the situation burned through even his stupidity and alcoholic haze. Kuroda moved the tip of the sword slightly.

"Well?"

"Up the monastery, up the monastery."

Think hard

Kuroda released his grip, the man stumbled away, blood pouring from the flesh wound in his neck. Kuroda cleaned the sword blade and slowly returned it to its scabbard. He sat down in the shade of the tree and planned his course of action. He gazed at the ripples in the stream as they caught the rays of the morning sun. He felt the ninja presence all around him, watching and waiting.

But the time was not right.

The watcher

CHAPTER FOURTEEN

DE BRIEFING

Shino removed the boy's clothes and with the pitcher of water, washed her body. As she bent over the low wooden bowl, her tiny breasts hung down, swaying slightly with the movements of her body as she washed the grime from her long hair. Having finished this task she stepped into the large wooden tub of hot water. The soothing liquid relaxed her tired muscles and she closed her eyes, enjoying the warmth on her skin.

After about twenty minutes, relaxed and refreshed, she stepped out of the tub and dried herself. She dressed in a sober blue kimono, gone were the false fineries of the Kanda house.

With her natural modesty; laid aside in the course of her mission; she dressed the collar of her kimono to cover the nape of her neck, the part of her body which had held the most sensual appeal for her clients. She then dressed her hair in a simple, practical style, thus dressed she was still bewitchingly beautiful.

Unlike the ninja priest who had undergone the ordeal of total recall, Shino had an appointment with the Master Tada and the inquisitors. She left the bathroom and walked down the familiar corridors of the fortress cave, until she came to the Master Tada's chamber. She entered, amongst the ninja, a woman was equal to a man for their missions were sometimes more harrowing and dangerous, unlike most of the outside world, where women took second place in daily affairs.

"Welcome Shino, it is good to see you after so long."

Her mission had lasted for about eighteen months,

Skills of the Ninja

during which time she had relayed the "pillow talk" of her carefully chosen clients to the Tomokatsu Ryu. Her means of transmission was her deaf mute servant, in reality also a Kunoichi ninja, who because of her plain looks, according to the standards of the time, was the ideal "back up" for Shino in her intelligence gathering.

"You are up to date with you intelligence reports I see Shino," said Master Tada gesturing to a scroll before him on the low table.

"The paymaster Okuda?"

Tada referred to her last client, whose ectasy was cut short by Shino's slow strangle.

"No problem," replied Shino.

"I completed the job very smoothly to Minoru's flute signal."

"Good," said Tada, "I am afraid that you have to go out again on another important mission."

"When?" she asked.

"Tomorrow morning," he replied, "but let me explain the urgency – we have an indirect link with General Tokugawa and his family. One of his minor samurai was killed in a test of skill with another samurai. It is strongly intimated that we must find the victor and dispose of him."

"What is the problem?" queried Shino.

"Well," said Tada, "this man is no ordinary man, he possesses some skill with the sword and until this very morning was in hiding with the old mountain dweller." (Thus did Tada refer to the master of the spirit of the wind, none but Kuroda knew his ultimate secret, his true name).

"But he will come out sometime," Shino replied.

"To be sure," Tada told her, "he is already out of hiding and somewhere near the Shotoji temple."

"Why not send Rinzo and his attack group?"

"Rinzo, along with his entire attack group are dead – surveillance team three found their bodies in a forest glade – it was like a battlefield."

"I see," said Shino, "what is the deadline?"

"Very short," said Tada, "the forces of General Tokugawa are massing. They will meet the Toyotomi army by the end of October. Although the importance of this mission is slight to the General Tokugawa, I feel that its outcome could seal the fate of the Tomokatsu Ryu. That is why we must succeed."

"What can I do to help?" Shino asked.

"Well, our samurai is quite a strange fellow – he has no name that we can find. But we do know that he has a wound on the right side of his chest and possibly more importantly,

Ninja training

that he has a tattoo of the war God Hachiman on his back.''

''On his back!'' Shino exclaimed increduously, for tattoos were for criminals and Ainu.

''We feel,'' Tada continued, ''that this may indeed be crucial. It could reveal a chink in his mental armour. Could it not?''

Tada looked at the two inquisitors who murmured their agreement.

''We believe you may well be the ideal weapon to pierce that armour.''

Ninja hooks

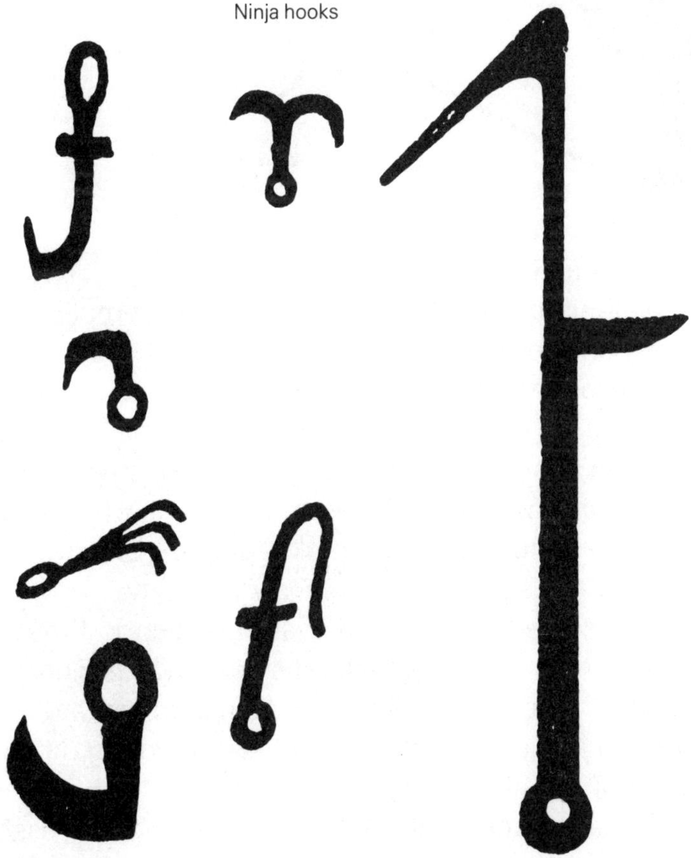

CHAPTER FIFTEEN

BATTLE FURY

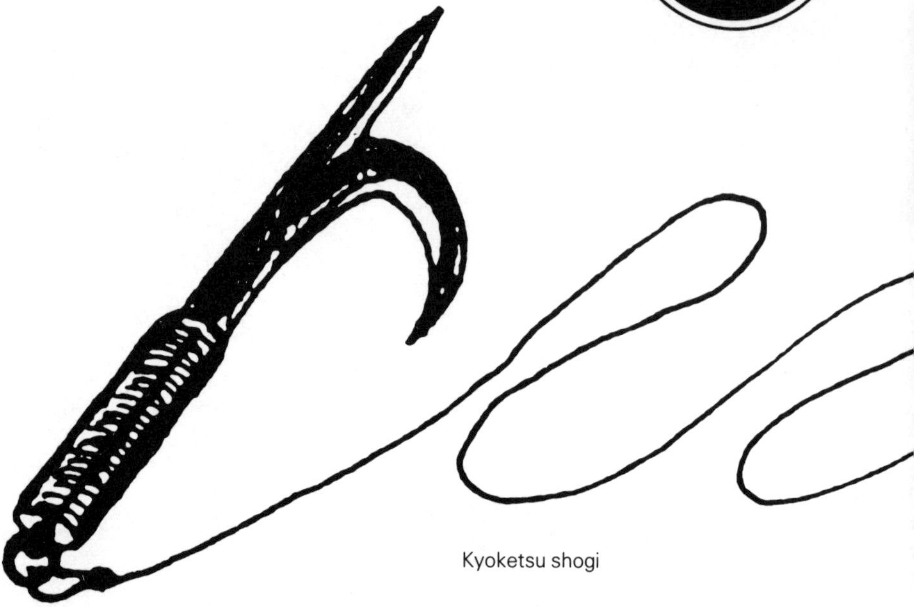

Kyoketsu shogi

With the prospect of finally avenging his lord, Kuroda strode the well-worn path towards the Shotoji temple, towards Miyake and towards . . .

The low branches brushed his face as he strode on with one purpose. He paid them no attention, his senses were becoming sharper, with every step. He felt the presence of the ninja around him – still keeping a distance. He felt almost like a character in the bunraku puppet theatre; closely observed the scenario relentlessly unfolding.

In the meditation hall, Miyake understood the significance of the great emptiness. His heart was laid bare and in its void formed the resolute acceptance of his fate. He was disturbed in his meditation by the same young monk, who first admitted him to the temple.

"Please excuse me, my lord Abbot Sochin wishes to

see you."

Miyake rose from the meditation posture and followed the monk, leaving the place where his enlightenment had clarified and become pure.

In the quiet seclusion of the Abbot's apartment, sat the master Sochin. He held the short stick, which in his hands became the sword of manjusri – the slayer of the ego.

Miyake entered and bowed –

"Sit!" said the Abbott.

Miyake sat, within striking distance of the stick.

"What is the significance of the great emptiness?"

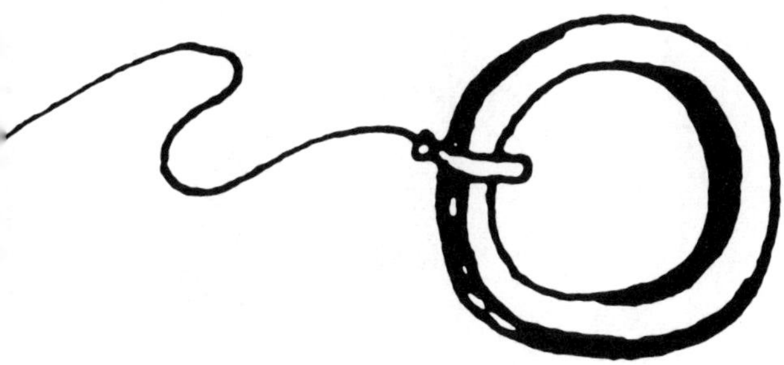

Miyake remained silent, his eyes fixed upon the eyes of the Abbot, cold and empty. The Abbot raised the stick in the manner of a sword.

Still Miyake did not move.

The sword of Manjusri flashed in the Abbot's hand. Miyake did not move.

The sword became a stick once more, it stopped, a hairsbreadth from Miyake's head.

Miyake did not move.

"Enter into the peace which knows no bounds" said the Abbot, "for you have achieved in this short time, the enlightenment which many strive their entire lives for. I do not question you of your reasons for coming, but I know that you must leave soon . . . "

Miyake did not answer.

Far away the faint ringing of the gatehouse bell – Kuroda

Kama

Ninja

had arrived. Then Miyake spoke to the Abbot Sochin for the last time –

"I hear that my fate has finally come to me, I must follow it to its course. I give up my swords to your safe-keeping."

With that, which to a samurai was the unendurable, Miyake left. He passed down the corridors, straightening the folds of his kimono and smoothing the ties of his hakama. He also carefully checked the knots of his chomage top knot – the mark of the samurai.

Outside the temple, Kuroda waited. He looked out on the thickly wooded hills and the mountains, almost a last goodbye.

Death was soon to come to this place – the natural courtyard in front of the temple with its dense forest background.

Whirling blade

Kuroda stood with his back turned to the temple. The small door within the gatehouse creaked as it slowly opened. He turned, as he did so he turned the sword in his sash, so that the blade edge faced downwards – ready for the single cut which would penetrate his opponent's heart.

Miyake walked from the shadows of the gatehouse, to within striking distance of Kuroda. Miyake entered the great silence. Kuroda waited; watching, probing. Miyake was unarmed. Still Kuroda waited. Then with a blinding flash – his left hand went to his sword hilt. It stopped short – "I cannot kill you Miyake" he said. "Your deed is your damnation, I cannot kill you."

In an unreal space of time, Kuroda heard the voice of the master of the spirit of the wind:

"The greatest victory is to win without fighting" the voice echoed.

"Kuroda turned and looked for his master, but there was no one there, save for Miyake. In their separate ways and for entirely different reasons, they had both achieved the pinnacle of enlightenment.

Then the burden hardest to bear, bore down upon Kuroda's spirit. Slowly he spoke, "If you are to live, the balance is set amiss. I must be true to my lord. The burden of obligation demands that honour be satisfied."

With this Kuroda turned away from Miyake. He dropped to his knees, drew his short sword and prepared to commit seppuku, the ritual suicide of the samurai. Thus would his debt to his lord be paid in full.

Almost at the same instant a large rock hit Miyake square in the forehead between his eyes. His skull fractured and with blood pumping from his wound he fell, dead.

The village roughs, led by the big ox charged into the courtyard brandishing sickles and staves. Kuroda was jolted

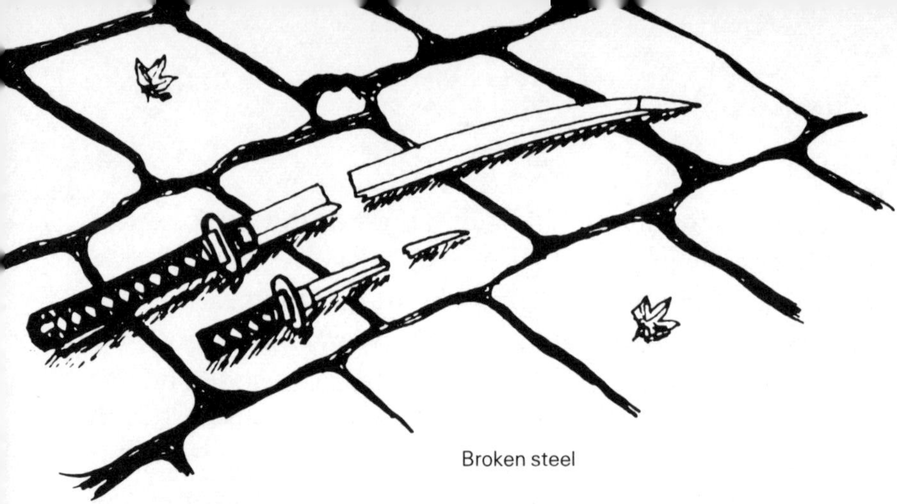

Broken steel

from his last rite. His super-honed senses attuned instantly to the situation. With his short sword in his hand he defended himself from the crazy onslaught. There were seven of them, they fought with animal ferocity. Kuroda blocked with the short sword as the sickle held by the big ox crashed down. Kuroda's blade broke under the fierce strength of the ox. His breath reeked of sake, for the roughs fought with the bravery of the bottle.

In an instant Kuroda leaped backward and drew his long sword. From the right came a whirling sickle from another of the men, big but not as big as the ox. Kuroda stepped straight, cutting Nashiwara – the pear splitter. An apt title, the man fell, cut from neck to groin. Kuroda leapt as a stave swung at him. He landed and cut the stave in two. His sword arced, then returned, cutting the stave's owner. Two more men rushed at him from behind. Kuroda spun. The force of his spinning carved the sword in a horizontal spiral upwards. The sword blade cut flesh, then bone – they fell.

The fifth rough sobered immediately and turned to run. Kuroda caught him with the pear splitter from behind. Then the sixth man was upon him. Kuroda dodged the stave, sharpened to a point and blackened in a fire to make any wound septic. His sword swung in the courtyard and the man stopped; his neck arteries severed.

Leaving only the big ox – he might have been stupid, but

Lock pick

he had natural, low cunning. Kuroda moved as he moved, never taking his eyes from him. Kuroda stepped over the fallen Miyake. The ox, thinking he had him at a disadvantage, charged in. His sickle slashed, through the air. Kuroda leaped straight at the ox, his sword pointed forward. It caught his opponent square in the chest, passing through the heart and out of his back. The man toppled, falling on the sword which was wrenched out of Kuroda's hand. As the ox hit the ground, the blade broke at the hilt with the deadweight.

Unarmed, but not defenceless, Kuroda probed the void for ninja attack. None came, their time was not ripe.

As Kuroda surveyed the scene, he looked down at the fallen – "Fools!" he said, with sincere regret. Sadly he turned his gaze to Miyake. In an all too brief moment they had forged an understanding and respect which death had sealed.

Kuroda would never know Miyake's reasons for killing their lord, and in a strange way, it no longer mattered. For in this moment, the scores were settled. Kuroda was a free man, unfettered from the bounds of obligation. He was, for the first time in his life – his own man.

The door of the temple opened and the Abbot walked out, flanked by his seniors. He looked with eyes untouched by emotion –

"Do not worry, we will take these fallen to our bosom – they will achieve true rest."

Kuroda looked puzzled, then realised that the depths of the void touched not only the warrior spirit, but also the gentle heart of the priest. Words of explanation did not matter.

A figure walked out from the temple, he drew alongside the Abbot. It was the young monk, in his hands he bore Miyake's swords. The Abbot took them and gave them to Kuroda.

"Bear them with honour" he said.

He turned and walked back into the temple, leaving Kuroda alone and free.

Ninja Fury

CHAPTER SIXTEEN

TWIGHLIGHT'S LAST GLEAMING

The edge of the precipice

Far away in the high mountains – the master of the spirit of the wind found the retreat he was looking for. In a natural cleft in the rock, flanked by sheer rock precipices.

He put down the few possessions which marked his life. He looked around his tiny plateau, feeling pleased. It was a fitting final resting place. He would not leave and he would never accept another pupil. He probed the world with his occult art. He saw Kuroda's progress to Shotoji and the confrontation with Miyake. The old master was pleased with Kuroda – he had learned well.

As night drew on – the old master boiled water to make tea. He sat on the edge of the rocky precipice. The valleys spread out before him like a map. In the far distance he saw the flickering glow of the forces of the Toyotomi and Tokugawa armies as they massed.

In the next few nights the fires were to become larger and more widespread as the Ashi-Garu footsoldiers made their decisions on which side they would fight. The old master felt the waves of pent-up aggression which bathed the area like a vast ocean. Soon the tidal wave would come and in the battle's fury, the force would dissipate.

The feeling was strong, the folly of it perturbed the old man. To take his mind off the inevitable he took up his brush

Twilight's last gleaming

Tanto

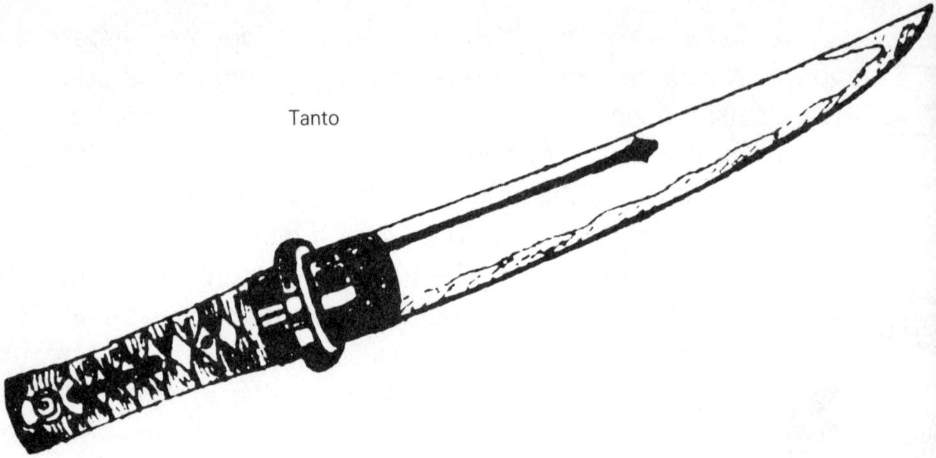

and in the flame from his tiny lamp, on a mountain top far away, he began to write –

"I set these words down for the use of my only true pupil, Kuroda Ichitaro, son of Kuroda Saburo, samurai of the Oka clan. Here I set down the principles of my way which I have named 'the spirit of the wind'. To Kuroda Ichitaro and his issue, I bequeath, this, my way, on the sixteenth day of October 1600, I am a retired samurai aged seventy one years."

The old man wrote – until the dawn light overtook the flame from the tiny lamp. He signed it and placed his personal seal upon it in red ink. He rolled the scroll up, wrapped it in an oiled cloth bag and secured it in the hollow handle of his naginata halberd. He set his spirit upon it, Kuroda would find it – the power of the wind spirit was great.

The old man rose and walked to the edge of the precipice. He sat down in the posture of meditation. In the distance, the smoke of fires hung like a low cloud.

On the horizon, the sun cut its edge brightly, splashing its red light on the old man's face. As the sun rose, the old man closed his eyes and as he sent the wind spirit forth, his heart stopped. He had chosen the method and moment of his death, but in death he was to grow far more powerful than in life.

CHAPTER SEVENTEEN

THE DARK FOREST

With the swords of Miyake thrust in his sash, the samurai Kuroda walked the byeways of the land – a free spirit for the first time in his life. Many times he had to stand aside as the horsemen of either faction galloped by, recruiting from the villages. The once quiet roads became highways of Ronin, the masterless samurai who, smelling battle, decided that a short violent life was better than a long peaceful one, and set out on a pilgrimage of steel.

Kuroda was not bothered by any of the wanderers, for they saw his ability and gave him a wide berth.

Kuroda felt an apprehension, not the awareness of his watchers, let them come. But on the night of the sixteenth day, he did not stay in a village, he needed the peace of the forest. He sat, without sleep, for the entire night. As the sun rose, he said to himself "it is over" and stood up. In his heart he knew that his master was dead, but felt no sadness, how could he mourn for that which cannot die? The old master's spirit would continue.

On the morning of the seventeenth, Kuroda entered a great forest, far away from the massing forces. He knew that he still needed solitude, but he also felt that the ninja were becoming bolder, a few times he caught a glimpse of a dark figure amongst the trees.

These trees thrust upwards towards the sky, leaving their roots far behind on the forest floor, their age comforted Kuroda's spirit.

In his heart he felt that confrontation was becoming a reality. Suddenly, a black figure dropped on to him from the high trees. He reacted swiftly and caught the figure, flipping

the body to the floor, he held the ninja in an immobilisation lock. Kuroda desperately wanted to know the reason for his pursuit – he must take this one alive – at least until he had made him talk.

Still holding the struggling ninja with one hand, he tore the black ninja mask off. A cascade of black hair tumbled out. As Kuroda gazed down at Shino's black eyes, his heart missed a beat, but he tried not to show how he was feeling. She struggled to reach a poisoned dart in the thigh of her ninja combat suit. Kuroda jabbed with his straightened thumb, under her left ear. She collapsed unconscious in one smooth action. Kuroda lifted her up and putting her across his shoulder, he began to walk through the forest.

He probed the void. The ninja presence felt extremely far away. He began to formulate the solution of Shino's single-handed attack upon him. It was clear that whoever controlled her, she was designed to kill him. The force created by a male attacker was different to that of a woman, it could have been the "trick" which would have finished Kuroda. He mused to himself that, prior to his knowledge of the wind spirit he would have been surprised, but not now.

Far away, in the depths of the forest, came the plaintiff sound of a bird. Kuroda paused, an actual song, or a ninja flanker? He continued to walk quickly. Shino's unconscious body felt weightless across his strong shoulders. After a while, he found what he had been looking for, a narrow

Climbing hook

Ninja throwing weapons

stream. Hitching up his hakama, he waded into its icy waters, up to his knees. Not even the most skilful ninja could track in water. He waded for about one mile then got out and struck off sharply north. As darkness came he saw the dark outline of an old hut, dilapidated but still wind and water proof. He checked it carefully, when he was sure that it was safe, he entered, placing Shino carefully in one corner. He

Soft words

Climbing spike

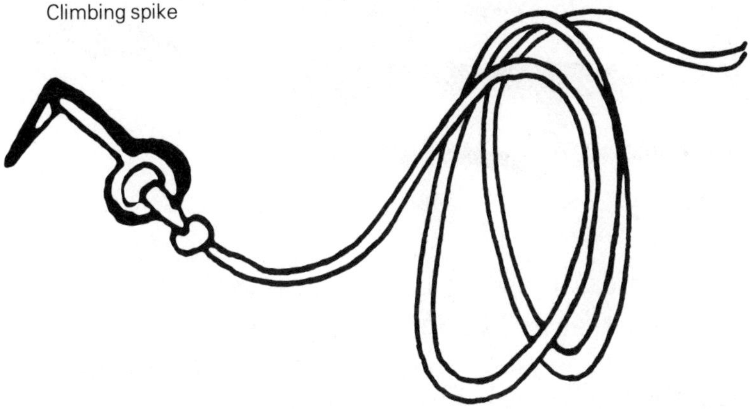

removed her armoury of weapons, amongst her equipment was a small lamp which he lit using the small piece of flint in its base. He left the hut and checked outside for any leakage of light, he stopped the gaps with brush wood. There came a stirring from inside. Kuroda dashed in, Shino opened her eyes, their gazes met. Kuroda's face was expressionless, Shino's a mirror of his, but a subtle chemistry of which they were both unaware, had begun to work.

The night passed swiftly, neither spoke. Kuroda had intended to question her, to find the answers to many questions, but now they seemed distant, foolish. Shino had intended, as ordered, to kill him, but now that too seemed foolish.

In the afternoon of the second day, Shino spoke, then like a flood tide she told Kuroda the complete story. Of how the ninja priest had promised the Tokugawa officials that the Tomokatsu Ryu ninja would find the samurai with the Hachiman tattoo. Of how the master Tada needed to gain status in the eyes of the Tokogawa heirachy. Her tale told, she stopped. Her emotions became too much for her and she began to cry. Shino, the courtesan, the kunoichi ninja,

Ninja weaponry

many times an assassin had come to the end of the blind madness that had been her ninja life.

Kuroda sensed the truth of her words and that she no longer presented any threat. She began to shake slightly, he reached forward and softly drew her to him. She stayed close, drained now of all hate. So came the dawning of an emotion she could not understand.

Days passed, they shared secret moments and enjoyed each other's company.

Kuroda said abruptly "I must find your master Tada, while he lives, we can never enjoy the safety which I desire. Time has been kind to us, in these few short days I feel I know you better than if we had lived together for twenty years."

"I know," said Shino, "I know, I cannot explain it, I did not want this to happen. But now that it has, I have never felt happier in my life – in fact I do not think that I have ever known happiness until this moment."

"You must leave, there is no place for you in my search for Tada. Take this," he gave her a square of paper which bore his personal seal, "travel to my clan. You will be safe there. Wait for me, I will come."

Shino's dark eyes flickered in his. She bound up her long hair and reversed her ninja combat suit into the clothes of a boy, her travelling disguise.

"I must go now, or I will never leave ." Sadly she rose and walked away, beginning her long journey to the home of Kuroda's clan. The seal would answer all questions, such was its power. As she walked away, neither of them knew

Ninja weaponry

then she bore the seed of Kuroda's child deep within her.

Kuroda turned away, the strong-willed warrior felt a sadness at their parting. Such was the spirit of the wind, it reflected all emotions truly. Night fell, still he sat silently within the hut, the place of the flourishing and blooming of their love.

Shino was now many miles away – on a journey which would take her a month. By its end she would be fully conscious of the truth which Kuroda could not yet know.

There was a strangeness, a flicker in the void. Kuroda remained motionless, Tada had found him.

In the darkness Kuroda delved deeper into the spirit of the wind than he had ever gone before. He sensed that Tada came alone. A dark shadow formed at the open doorway. With snake like speed Kuroda reached for one of Shino's fragmentation grenades. He threw it. A brief light, an explosion and a shriek of pain as Tada caught the full force of the blast.

Then Tada was gone. Kuroda rose and began to track the master of the Tomokatsu ninja.

Ninja weaponry

CHAPTER EIGHTEEN

THE WORLD'S END

Blood trickled down the ninja master Tada's left arm. There were jagged pieces of Shino's fragmentation grenade from wrist to shoulder. The chain mail surcoat which he wore under the red/black combat suit had prevented severe wounding, but nevertheless his injuries created a blinding white pain in his mind. He concentrated hard on the Kankuji mind control, the pain lessened almost to a pleasurable blur. Only his determination spurred him on.

He knew that Kuroda was closing fast, the tables had been turned, the hunter had become the hunted.

The thick forest became thinner, the old trees gave way to younger trees, then to saplings. Tada rushed onwards in a furious attempt to put as much distance between himself and Kuroda as possible. A dull roar reached his ears, becoming deafening as he gained the brow of the hill – the scream of men and horses as they fell under the merciless hail of the Tokugawa matchlock guns.

Battle reality

Tada paused for a second as he surveyed the carnage of the battlefield of the place known as Sekigahara. The valley was awash with the blood of both sides, the cavalry were used up, now came the killing time. The ragged armies of the Ashi-Garu footsoldiers closed on each other, breaking ranks, they plied their deadly trade. Companions of another time pitted against each other for the highest reward. Solid lines of men gave way under the storm of sword and spear. Great deeds of bravery and cowardice took place on both sides that day.

Drawing his sword with his good right arm, Tada began

his running descent into the vale of blood. Kuroda could not hope to find him now – but as the master Tada had observed only a few short weeks ago, "Here was no ordinary man."

Tada rushed across the churned up mud of the once pleasant valley. A crowd of Toyotomi Ashi-Garu closed in on the black clad figure. Twenty against one, an easy plunder. There was a blinding flash, then a cloud of orange smoke. The Ashi-Garu fell to the ground, clutching at their faces as a combined fragmentation and smoke grenade exploded at head height. A dark figure leaped high through the orange fog.

High up on one hill, the General Tokugawa, in full Oyoroi battle armour, bearing the hollyhock crest of his family, surveyed the scene. In his right hand he held the gunpai battle fan with the order for battle written upon it in delicate black characters. With faint interest he observed the flash and the orange smoke which billowed out on the left flank. There was a terrible beauty, a structured order to mass death, he thought to himself. His mind then turned to the massing Toyotomi cavalry coming hard and fast from the centre column. He raised the gunpai and his matchlock fusiliers fired a volley. The cavalry disintegrated into a flailing mass of horses and men. Armour tore apart and battle pennants tattered in the face of merciless musket fire.

On the opposite hill, the General Ishida of the Toyotomi gazed with resolute acceptance at his fate. His last columns

Arrow head

of cavalry gone the way of the rest; he called his samurai lieutenants together for the final stand – there would be no surrender.

As the ballet of battle danced on, Kuroda had left the forest and was running up the low hill. His mind was troubled for he sensed the pain and suffering within the void as thousands gave up life. Reaching the crest of the hill he saw the terrible beauty. He had been a part of such a scene many times before but this time it was not his fight. He must find Tada. He would cross the battlefield without drawing his sword, unless absolutely necessary. He was a free man now and his battle was elsewhere.

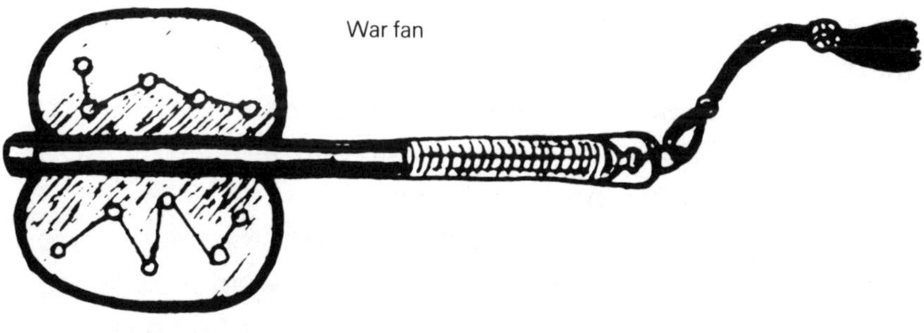

War fan

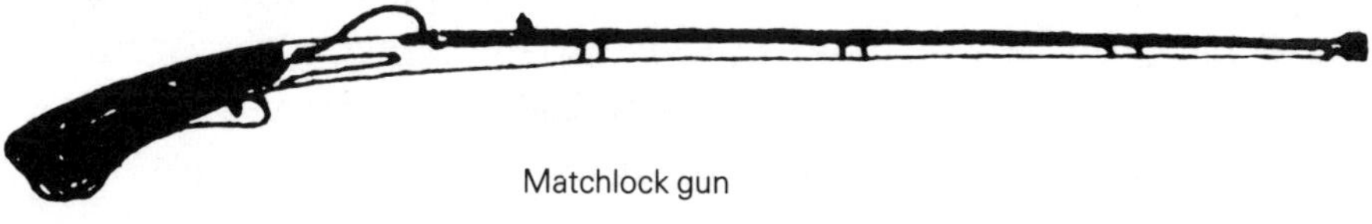

Matchlock gun

Battle pennant

He rushed past a group of Ashi-Garu – their faces masks of blood, they staggered around almost drunkenly until picked off by the stragglers, the dregs of the battlefield. Now Kuroda was in the thick of the fighting. He dodged past large and small groups of fighting men. To his right a horse vainly tried to rise, but both its front legs were broken. It pinned down the armoured samurai, once its master, until a cowardly Ashi-Garu caught hold of the samurai by the helmet bowl and thrust a bloody dagger deep into his neck. He moved no more.

Tada had almost crossed the battlefield by this time. His supply of throwing stars was nearly exhausted as he fought his way through both Toyotomi and Tokugawa ranks. In the front line was the harshest fighting and Tada, with one arm useless, his sword gone, fought like a demon. The ten thousand power chain whirled and scythed as a samurai in full armour bore down upon him. A spray of iron filings, from Tada's now empty scabbard, blinded his attacker and the ten thousand power chain found its mark. The samurai dropped to the mud. Tada threw the useless scabbard away. Two stars, the chain and a single fragmentation grenade, were all the remnants of his personal armoury.

Kuroda was within the middle ground of the fighting. He had not yet drawn his sword, he had managed thus far, to avoid conflict. Then he was confronted by a boy of about sixteen years of age. He bore the topknot of the samurai. His lightweight armour and kimono were spattered with blood, not his own. He blocked Kuroda's path. Kuroda sidestepped; the youth too, sidestepped, blocking his path yet again. Kuroda used the occult power of the spirit of the wind.

The battlefield

The rope bridge

"I will not fight you, I have business elsewhere."

"Fight me!" screamed the boy.

"I will not fight" he pushed with the wind spirit. The boy's mind froze for a brief second. That was enough – Kuroda was past him. The boy looked around in wonderment; started to give chase, thought better of it and rushed off to fight another day.

Sensing the void like a hungry tiger, Kuroda picked his way through the deadly maze. Looking up, he saw a dark shadow moving up the closely wooded hill, not a hundred paces away. It must be Tada. With no conflict, he had passed quickly through the carnage. But Tada, who had fought every inch of the way, had been slowed down, and now he was within sight.

The exertion of the Kankuji mind control was telling on Tada. As he raced up the hill, running in and out of the tree strewn path, sharp jets of pure pain racked his nerve system as the Kankuji lessened its power. Then, with redoubled effort, took over again. Tada paused, his breathing heavy, he looked around and down, to see Kuroda pounding across the empty space at the foot of the hill. With a super-human effort, he threw his last grenade, it bounced harmlessly against the trees next to Kuroda's head. Whether this was due to the protection of the wind spirit, or the fact that the fuse was soaked with Tada's blood – no one will ever know.

Kuroda did not break the rhythm of his strides as he thundered up the hill towards his quarry. Tada turned and fled to the top of the hill, across a narrow ridge, which gave way to a yawning chasm – he was trapped. However an escape did offer itself. Fifty paces away was a hastily constructed rope bridge, built by the Toyotomi engineers to carry vital supplies. It was guarded on the far side by a single Ashi-Garu, holding a short-bladed spear. Silently Tada drew his throwing star, it flew and fell short, the next and last star caught the guard under the left ear, he collapsed, choking on his own blood.

The abyss

The rope bridge swayed gently in the breeze as Tada's feet padded across its wooden planks. He had reached half way when a voice boomed out, "Stop!" It was Kuroda. Tada stopped and turned, he calmed his breathing.

Kuroda removed his swords, placed them lightly on the ground and walked purposefully onto the swaying bridge. His mind was calm, concerned only with the task in hand, no fear of death, or life. He walked on. The sound of the rushing torrent in the chasm filled his brain as its black waters tumbled and crashed to the sea.

Tada, sensing the moment, drew his last line of attack—the ten thousand power chain. It snaked its way lazily toward Kuroda, as if time had slowed. Kuroda ducked his head, the chain fell uselessly to the ground beyond the rope bridge.

There could be no turning or running now, this was man to man, a final confrontation to the death.

With the last ounce of effort in his body, Tada, master ninja of the Tomokatsu Ryu, leaped into the air and straight at Kuroda. Kuroda also jumped to meet the attack and the two men locked in mid-air.

As they crashed together with bone-shattering force, the master ninja Tada butted Kuroda with all his strength. Their heads crashed and Kuroda saw flashes of light, then a brief velvet blackness as the force of his enemy's steel-tipped head band rang through his brain. Blood flowed into Kuroda's eyes.

Then the fates dealt their final card. The gentle wind which had softly blown the rope bridge, gusted stronger. Locked in a grim embrace, the two men dropped into emptiness as the rope bridge was blown away. They tumbled over and over, the swirling black waters rushing up to meet them. Then, in a brief instance, the very forces of time and nature stopped in their course.

Icy cold fingers gripped tightly around Kuroda's shoulders and in his mind he heard the calm, gentle voice of the master of the spirit of the wind.

"Not yet Kuroda my son. Death shall not have you." Kuroda was ripped out of Tada's deadly embrace, and the ninja master plunged alone to the icy cradle of the river far below.

Time resumed its natural course. Kuroda was back on the rope bridge, the salty taste of his own blood on his lips. He looked down as Tada's body was swept away in the foaming water.

"We shall meet another day, another place" he vowed softly "and I shall see you dead."

Kuroda turned, and walked back to where his swords lay, he thrust them through his sash and strode off on the long journey to Shino.

"THE SPIRIT OF THE WARRIOR
HOLDS THE SHADOW OF THE NINJA"
(from the Secret Scrolls of the Tomokatsu Ryu)

Other Titles published by Dragon Books

Kanazawa's Karate
By Hirokazu Kanazawa 8th Dan

Nunchaku Dynamic Training
By Hirokazu Kanazawa 8th Dan

Advanced Shotokan Kata (In preparation)
By Enoeda Keinosuke 8th Dan
Volume 1
Bassai Dai : Kanku-Dai : Jion : Empi : Hangetsu
Volume 2
Bassai-Sho : Kanku-Sho : Jiin : Gankaku : Sochin
Volume 3
Tekki-Nidan : Tekki-Sandan : Jitte : Chinte : Unsu :
Nijushiho : Gojushiho-Dai : Gojushiho-Sho :
Meikyo (Rohai) Wankan

Dynamic Kicking Method (In preparation)
By M. Shiomitsu 7th Dan

Dragon Books Ltd
10 Thornbury Rd Isleworth Middx TW7 4HG
London England